GODDESS FOR A N

Adam knelt before Cat, his head on a level with her bared breasts. Slowly he placed the silver concho belt he had created around her waist and snapped the clasp shut.

"Now," he said, helping her release her skirt and frothy petticoat. The garments slid silkily over the lush curve of her hips and fell in a foamy heap at her bare feet.

"You look like a moon goddess," Adam said huskily. "All ivory and silver except for your flaming hair."

Deliciously his lips covered her breasts with kisses, and when she pulled him close, his hands moved slowly over her hips and down the smooth contours of her legs in soft, sensuous circles.

Then his strong hands were at her waist, tugging at the belt clasp, the thin veneer of civilization dropping away from him, and then from her, as she welcomed him and they began to move together in the ancient rhythm. . . .

MARIANNE CLARK lives in a converted barn among the green meadows and lakes of Michigan. She loves the company of family and friends, walking on deserted beaches, and Irish music. When not writing, she relaxes by painting in acrylics or playing the guitar, and she admits to collecting antique inkwells, old medical books, and the occasional stray cat. She is President of the Greater Detroit Chapter of Romance Writers of America.

Dear Reader:

The editors of Rapture Romance have only one thing to say—thank you! At a time when there are so many books to choose from, you have welcomed ours with open arms, trying new authors, coming back again and again, and writing to us of your enthusiasm. Frankly, we're thrilled!

In fact, the response has been so great that we now feel confident that you are ready for more stories which explore all the possibilities that exist when today's men and women fall in love. We are proud to announce that we will now be publishing six titles each month, because you've told us that four Rapture Romances simply aren't enough. Of course, we won't substitute quantity for quality! We will continue to select only the finest of sensual love stories, stories in which the passionate physical expression of love is the glorious culmination of the entire experience of falling in love.

And please keep writing to us! We love to hear from our readers, and we take your comments and opinions seriously. If you have a few minutes, we would appreciate your filling out the questionnaire at the back of this book, or feel free to write us at the address below. Some of our readers have asked how they can write to their favorite authors, and we applaud their thoughtfulness. Writers need to hear from their fans, and while we cannot give out addresses, we are more than happy to forward any mail.

Happy reading!

Robin Grunder
Rapture Romance
New American Library
1633 Broadway
New York, NY 10019

APACHE TEARS

by
Marianne Clark

RAPTURE ROMANCE
NEW AMERICAN LIBRARY
TIMES MIRROR

PUBLISHER'S NOTE

This novel is a work of fiction. Names, characters, places, and incidents are either the product of the author's imagination or are used fictitiously, and any resemblance to actual persons, living or dead, events, or locales is entirely coincidental.

NAL BOOKS ARE AVAILABLE AT QUANTITY DISCOUNTS
WHEN USED TO PROMOTE PRODUCTS OR SERVICES.
FOR INFORMATION PLEASE WRITE TO PREMIUM MARKETING DIVISION,
THE NEW AMERICAN LIBRARY, INC., 1633 BROADWAY,
NEW YORK, NEW YORK 10019.

Copyright © 1983 by Marianne Willman

All rights reserved

SIGNET, SIGNET CLASSIC, MENTOR, PLUME, MERIDIAN AND NAL BOOKS
are published by The New American Library, Inc.,
1633 Broadway, New York, New York 10019

First Printing, November, 1983

1 2 3 4 5 6 7 8 9

PRINTED IN THE UNITED STATES OF AMERICA

*For Katie and Sand,
who live over the Rainbow Bridge*

Chapter One

Mabel Walker, owner of the spacious gallery with its mirrored walls and columns and three enormous crystal chandeliers, sidled up to Catriona. "Do you see who's here? It's quite a coup for you!"

Cat turned around and froze at the sight of a tall, raven-haired man with startling blue eyes and a bronzed complexion. She recognized him immediately from his pictures. He was Adam Hawk, the famous Navaho silversmith whose work was internationally renowned and whose private life was considered to be an intriguing mystery by all. Cat's heart beat a little faster. Adam Hawk, at her first gallery show! At the moment, he stood beside an ebony pedestal displaying several of her silver bracelets and she could not help staring at him.

"Where did he get those blue eyes?" she whispered almost to herself.

"Remember, his mother, Beatrice Longshadow, is half-Navaho and half-Irish," Mabel answered. "I heard her sing at the Met once before she retired. I've always wondered why she disappeared from the scene so suddenly."

While the man examined Cat's handwrought jewelry, she examined him. Nervously, she brushed away a red-gold tendril that had escaped from the side of her neat chignon. "What do you think, Mabel? Does he like my work?" Although Cat was proud of her jewelry, this was her first major exhibition and she could not help succumbing to a certain amount of nervousness.

"His face certainly doesn't give anything away, does it?" Mabel replied.

Cat watched his movements in one of the mirrored pillars, pretending not to look as Adam Hawk prowled among the gold and ebony cases with leisurely grace.

In his black suit and black Stetson with the feathered band, he stood out starkly against the thick white carpeting and the crystal and gold interior of Detroit's Walker Gallery. A silver cuff bracelet covered one strong wrist and a finely wrought Concho belt wound around his slim waist. He should have looked out of place, Cat thought, but he didn't. From the moment he had entered the gallery, his height and electric presence had commanded the room.

"I wish he'd smile or frown, or *something*," Cat mumbled to herself. She'd seen Hawk's pieces in museums and shows and had always greatly admired his work; indeed, he had been one of the major influences in the development of her own style. She nibbled her lip in anxiety. Would he understand what she was trying to say with the jewelry in this show? This exhibit was very important to Cat, both professionally and personally.

In the past six months since she had ended her

relationship with Lawrence, Cat had concentrated on rebuilding her confidence. She had restructured her sense of self carefully, bit by bit, and only her work, her skill as an artisan held it in place. If her show was a failure, it might all fall apart—and then what would be left of Catriona Frazer, she wondered? Pieces of wire, molten puddles of gold, and a handful of loose stones and polished gems? Right now, all her self-esteem, her very future rode on this show and its acceptance by the critics and the public.

"He's coming this way." Mabel poked Cat in the ribs with a discreet elbow. "Go talk to him," she whispered as she swept off.

Cat turned around. Hawk was scrutinizing a necklace of gold-veined silver leaves. It was one of Cat's favorite pieces. At last he made a small, almost grudging sound of approval before moving closer to where Cat stood. She liked the way he moved, and as he picked up a bracelet of twisted gold set with carnelian, she noticed his long hands were finely shaped and he had the sensitive blunt-tipped fingers of an artist or musician.

She held her breath as he inspected the bangle somewhat cursorily. She still couldn't read his expression, but she had a sinking feeling of disappointment: he didn't like it. She didn't know how she knew, but she knew it!

He noticed her then, his gaze flickering over the fine bones and delicate coloring of her face. He seemed to like what he saw, for his look softened and his firmly chiseled lips widened in a slight smile. In fact, he seemed more interested in Cat than in her jewelry.

"What do you think of the bracelet?" she asked, the words catching in her suddenly dry throat.

Hawk looked directly at her and the intense, clear blue of his eyes dazzled her. They were like the sky on a perfect summer day. As he swung around to face Cat, a subtle aroma of sandalwood and amber enveloped her.

"It's quite . . . pretty," he said casually, relegating it in her mind to the status of costume jewelry.

Catriona felt as if she'd been slapped in the face. *Pretty!* How dare he dismiss her skill and efforts so patronizingly. Resentment and indignation flooded through her. Who did he think he was? Did he think her work was inferior because she lived in Detroit instead of Phoenix or Sedona? Well, she was good. Damn good.

At her sharp intake of breath, Hawk looked at her more closely. His glance locked with hers, his blue eyes arrested by the flare of fire in her green ones, and she challenged him boldly. His eyes roved over her blaze of red hair and ivory skin, taking in her small, high-bridged nose and soft, rosy lips with a gleam of appreciation. Then suddenly his look changed to consternation as he finally guessed her identity. His mobile mouth twisted in a rueful smile.

"Catriona Frazer?" he said. It was a statement and held no hint of apology.

"Yes, I'm Cat Frazer." Her eyes sparkled dangerously. "You don't seem impressed with my work, Mr. Hawk."

Neither her words nor the fact that she knew his identity fazed him one bit. He looked at her, then at the bracelet that still dangled from his large bronzed hand.

"It is *pretty*," he answered, his voice regretful and . . . what? Disappointed? He made no move to leave, but stood watching her intently.

Cat bristled. With great effort, she controlled her demon temper and kept her voice low and steady. "Is that all you have to say? That's two years of my life that you've just dismissed as 'pretty'!" Bright color suffused her cheeks, making her green eyes glow a dark emerald in contrast. She knew she was on the verge of making a scene, but it didn't matter. Nothing mattered at the moment but this master silversmith's rejection of her work as serious and significant art. She took a deep breath and tried to seem calm, unaware that her eyes betrayed her.

"I put my heart and soul into this exhibit, and I think it deserves much more than a backhanded compliment!"

He looked at her, a long steady look from those startling azure eyes, and his lips curled in a strange smile. When he spoke, his words were measured and deliberate. "Your 'heart and soul,' Miss Frazer? I think not. Right now, I can see the *real* Catriona Frazer blazing with passion before me." He gestured at the display cases near them. "But I see none of that passion here."

Catriona was speechless with hurt and fury. This

man, whose work she'd so long admired, was arrogant to the point of rudeness. Why, he even ignored her technical skills. She made an impatient gesture.

Suddenly Adam Hawk's hand shot out and captured her right wrist. She felt his warm touch burning like a brand into her flesh. His eye flashed with a deep inner light.

"Did you design that?" he demanded, pointing with his other hand to the silver and copper ring that coiled like a living vine around her finger. It was the ring she'd crafted after her recent and disturbing phone call from Lawrence. She tried to pull her arm away, but Hawk held it in a vise-like grip.

"Yes," she said with a toss of her proud head. "I designed and made it."

"When?" His eyes searched her face.

"A month ago," she answered, torn between anger and bewilderment. His grasp relaxed and he touched the ring gently, his face creased in a smile that showed his strong white teeth.

"In this piece I can see your spirit, your 'heart and soul,' as you put it."

She caught the excitement in his voice, and this time the bloom that came to her cheeks was from the pleasure his words gave her. She was irrevocably caught up in this man with the compelling voice and artist's hands.

"In this ring," Hawk continued softly, "I can see love and doubt and passion . . . and pain . . ." He seemed hypnotized, so intense was his scrutiny, and yet he held her hand as lightly as if it were a rare butterfly. Cat felt as if he'd looked into the past or read her mind, and he caught the tiny tremor of shock that ran through her.

"Am I right?" he asked in a low voice. She nodded. He still held her wrist while his other hand supported hers in a touch that was at once detached and sensual. That strange contact stirred up sensations that Cat had tried to suppress, to forget for a long time.

Hawk took in a long breath. He let go of her wrist, then raised her hand and surprised her by pressing his warm lips to it in a kind of salute. The answering tingle that ran along her arm and down her spine frightened Cat. She had promised herself when she broke off her relationship with Lawrence that no man would ever be able to affect her in the same way, making her confused and light-headed by his very presence. Yet, now, in a matter of minutes, Adam Hawk had shattered her complaisance, overwhelming her with sensations and emotions she no longer felt equipped to handle.

She looked around in a near panic and noticed that several people in the gallery were watching them with great interest, including Mabel Walker and Cat's roommate, Angelica Smith. The gallery owner threw a gratified look in Cat's direction. Angel's expression made it clear that she couldn't have cared less about Hawk's identity; she was obviously bowled over by his good looks.

Cat signaled for one of them to rescue her. She wanted someone, anyone, to interrupt her conversation with this disturbing man so she could walk away with dignity.

When she turned back to Hawk, she found his eyes riveted on her face, and a frown marred her smooth forehead. He looked down at the nearby display and idly fingered a massive man's ring covered with hundreds of minute gold beads and inlaid with slabs of lapis lazuli.

"And is that *pretty*, too, Mr. Hawk?" she heard herself say without conscious will.

He picked up the ring and hefted it in his palm a moment, then checked the construction and finish on the inside of the band.

"A good design. Precise workmanship. A light touch. But nothing more." His eyes challenged her, then he sighed and replaced the ring.

Catriona's face drained of all color. "That ring won me second place and a two-thousand-dollar grant at the last regional Metalworkers and Craftsmen Guild's Show. Are you a fool, Mr. Hawk, or did you come here tonight just to laugh at me?" she hissed. "Are you here to put down some provincial midwestern silversmith who has the audacity to think she belongs in your field? Funny, from the honesty in your work, I didn't think you'd be the kind of man to let all the praise go to your head. Apparently I was wrong!"

Once, she would have given anything for a few minutes with Adam Hawk, the master metalworker who had inspired her to reach for more creative heights; now, as she lost the remnants of her temper, she felt hurt, betrayed, and disillusioned. She wished the floor would open beneath their feet and swallow one of them—preferably *him*!

She swept away, making toward the door to Mrs. Walker's elegant private office, but he was right on her heels as she crossed the threshold. Cat whirled around and tried to close the door, but he wedged his tall frame in the opening, pushed his way through, and then firmly closed the door behind him. When she realized that he wouldn't budge, she simply turned her back on him and worked to regain her composure. She didn't hear a sound, but suddenly his hands were on her shoulder, forcing her around to face him.

"Do you always sneak up on people?" she gasped.

"Do you always go off like a ten-megaton bomb?" he answered.

She raised her clenched hands—to do what, she didn't quite know—and he imprisoned both her wrists in his large hands.

"Let me go, dammit!" she demanded.

"Only if you promise to hold still for a few minutes while I talk to you, instead of darting here and there like a demented dragonfly."

She stopped struggling and tilted her head up to meet his gaze with what little dignity she could muster, and then stopped. She hadn't realized how close he was, how tall he was. Despite her indignation, she felt a womanly stirring of response to his vital magnetism, a response that she instantly quelled. His eyes seemed impossibly blue as his bronze skin flushed darker and some unidentifiable emotion flickered over his face for a split second. He lowered her hands, but kept them in his.

"Will you be still and listen a minute if I let you go?"

"Yes," she snapped, wanting to put some physical distance between herself and this man who affected her so strangely . . . and so strongly.

He dropped her wrists and eyed her warily.

"Why are you looking at me like that?" she demanded. "Hasn't anyone else told you how rude and arrogant you are? Are you afraid I'll tell you 'the Emperor has no clothes'?"

"Afraid of *you*?" And then he began to laugh. His laughter was spontaneous and somehow infectious. "Not in the way you mean," he said with a wry smile.

Cat was surprised and thrown off balance by his reaction. She'd expected anger, resentment, even disdain, but not good-natured laughter and warm smiles.

"Don't look so astonished," Hawk continued. "I'm told that I'm rude and arrogant at least once a day, so why should I take offense?"

Cat stared at him. The person she saw now was as open, as disarming and warm as she had pictured Adam Hawk to be from the pieces of his silverwork that she had seen and touched and admired. Which was the real man? He changed like a chameleon from one moment to the next.

"Look," Hawk said, putting an end to Cat's lapse into silence. "I didn't mean to be rude, and that's certainly not the reason I came here tonight. But you asked my opinion and I gave it. Perhaps too freely, but I stand by my words. You're good, but not as good as you could be. As you *should* be. You've lost that lyrical, fanciful way of looking at the world, at yourself, that made your earlier work so remarkable."

"You're wrong," Cat answered hotly. "I've learned a lot this past year. My skills and techniques are better than they ever were." She remembered the words of a Chicago art critic: "Miss Frazer shows increasing sophistication in every polished line and curve of her latest pieces . . ."

Instead of answering, he reached into the inner pocket of his suitcoat and brought out a small object wrapped in a colorful handkerchief of silk paisley. The cloth fell away to reveal a small octagonal hand mirror framed in silver, the back decorated with a graceful narcissus done in the flowing Art Nouveau style of the 1930s.

Cat was astounded. She'd sold the mirror in Toronto three years before.

"Where did you get my mirror?" she asked breathlessly.

Hawk didn't answer her directly; instead, he ran a long lean finger over the silver flower. "When I first saw this mirror," he said, "I took one look at the narcissus and knew the artist who made it had to have a delightful sense of humor." He held it out to her and she took it, almost reluctantly. She was glad he'd recognized her little joke, playing on the legend of beautiful Narcissus, who became enamored of his own reflection and died, heart broken, of unrequited love.

The silver was warm from being carried close to his body, and holding it, Cat felt as if he'd touched her, as if her acceptance of the mirror from his hand had closed some kind of electrical circuit and captured them both in a current of sudden intimacy. She almost dropped the mirror.

"In other words," she said when she was able to speak calmly, "you think my recent work doesn't compare favorably with my earlier pieces?" She tried to keep her voice level, but heard the slight quiver.

Hawk stepped closer and took one of her hands gently in his, searching her face with his piercing eyes.

"What happened?" His voice was low and gentle. "I thought at first that maybe you'd become smug and self-satisfied about your work, or that you'd sold out and were going after the money. I even thought that maybe you didn't care anymore, but now I know that's not it at all." He sighed softly. "So, what happened?" He sounded so concerned and sincere that for an instant Cat wanted to lay her head on his shoulder and pour out all the pain and loneliness of the past few months.

Instead, she stiffened and pulled her hand away. This time he made no move to restrain her. She didn't dare let him get too close, didn't dare let anyone break through the fragile wall of her self-control and newly built self-assurance.

"Look," he said when no answer was forthcoming. "It's almost time for the gallery to close. Let's go somewhere and catch a bite to eat and talk about this."

Cat walked across the room and turned away from him. "There's nothing to talk about," she said in a low voice. There was no sound behind her. Had he moved? She turned back. Hawk was still standing where she'd left him, his blue eyes hooded as he shrewdly observed her.

"I can help you," he answered. Instantly her temper flamed.

"I don't need your help. And I don't want your condescension. Just get out of here. Please, just leave me alone." That was all that she wanted, to be alone with her anger and her thoughts and her tears.

Adam Hawk carefully placed one of his cards on the corner of the desk. "I *can* help you," he told her quietly. "And I think you can help me. I came here tonight to talk about a job that might interest you. You wouldn't have to work at the Detroit Art Institute anymore; you could devote all your time to your craft. And despite what I saw here tonight—or rather didn't see—I still think you're the right person for the position."

Catriona glared at the man. "This is ridiculous. One minute you insult my work, and the next you're offering me a job."

"Here's my card," he said. "I'll be at the Westin Hotel in the Renaissance Center through Friday. Call me when you cool down." With that, he left, shutting the door firmly behind him.

Change her mind! *Never*, Catriona thought emphatically, dashing away the tears on her cheeks. Hell would freeze solid before she changed her mind! But as she wiped her eyes and freshened her makeup, her anger fizzled under the rising waves of curiosity.

What kind of job opportunity? It didn't make any sense. She could never work with Adam Hawk, not after the disparaging remarks he'd made about her exhibit. And what of all the work she'd done to prove her independence, to show that she could exist as a person in her own right, away from the all-consuming flame of Lawrence's brilliance? The struggle had been long and painful, and knowing that Lawrence didn't understand had added to that pain. And no arrogant Indian, no matter how good a silver-smith he was, could make her believe that she wasn't one of the best!

She looked at her reflection in the silver mirror and saw there were no traces of tears or anger showing. She started to leave the mirror on Mabel's desk, but for some reason she rewrapped it in the silk square and dropped it into her purse. And when she started out of the office, she paused, picked up Hawk's card, and placed it carefully in her purse next to the silver mirror.

Chapter Two

Catriona returned to the exhibit area, hoping to steal away after a hasty farewell to Mabel. She wanted to go home and lick her wounds, but fate was against her.

"Kitty, darling!" The low voice with precise British tones caught her up short. She turned and her worst fears were confirmed.

"Lawrence! What are you doing in town? I thought you were in London." Instantly she was clasped in his hard embrace, and the remembered scent of cherry-wood pipe tobacco and Aramis cologne surrounded her.

"I came to see your first show," he replied, although his eyes were for her and not the exhibition of jewelry. "So, now at last you have achieved what you wanted." His expression grew speculative. "We can pick things up where we left off . . ."

Although the words were casual, even offhanded, Cat heard a note of uncertainty and was surprised. She had never known him to be unsure of anything, especially when it concerned his work—or his women.

"What's the matter?" she asked. "Has Mara left you again?" Instantly she was ashamed of her childish jab, but he seemed delighted with her comeback.

"I'm glad to see I can still make you jealous, Kitty." His smug smile irritated her.

"No, I'm not jealous, Lawrence," she said, sidestepping the arm that slid possessively around her waist. "That was very rude of me. I'm sorry." She wasn't, but it never hurt to practice keeping her temper under better control.

Lawrence looked down at her appraisingly. "Oh? Has my sharp-clawed kitten finally grown up? I'll have to call you Cat now, like your friends do."

Yes, Cat thought, I have grown up. At least enough to see Lawrence as a human being and not some omnipotent god. Looking at him now, she was amazed to think she had ever seen him in that light.

"Lawrence, you don't have to call me *anything*. We agreed not to see each other." She shook her head. "It's too soon for us to be friends, and too late for us to be anything else."

"Such a pity," he said, leaning forward a little to inhale the perfume of her hair. He straightened up as angry sparks flared in her green irises. For a moment he looked like a little boy who'd just been told he wasn't going to the circus after all. His lips turned up in the crooked, charming smile that had melted her heart a hundred times before, but it didn't affect her as it had in the past. Despite her irritation she found herself smiling back.

"You haven't changed at all," she told him. "Still the aloof, mysterious author with a small mischievous boy lurking just below the surface."

"Guilty as charged. Now, let's go have a late dinner." He wandered over to a display and turned to study a necklace inlaid with mother-of-pearl as if the matter were settled.

Cat laughed, half in exasperation, half in rueful amusement. He was the same old Lawrence: clever, impulsive, and as unconsciously demanding and dominating as ever. He turned back to her with one of his quick, characteristic movements.

"I have just the place for a celebration," he told her, and Cat saw the gleam of deviltry in his eyes. He'd planned to spend this whole evening with her, she knew, down to the last little detail.

"Where?" the word slipped out of her spontaneously.

"Philadelphia!" he exclaimed like a king bestowing a boon on his handmaiden.

"Oh, Lawrence." She laughed and shook her head. "Why on earth would I want to go to Philadelphia for dinner?"

"Hoagies," he answered, as if the word explained everything.

"What?"

"Hoagies! Submarines! Philadelphia fried-steak sandwiches with onions. Delicious. My latest enthusiasm," he added needlessly, and Cat, who had cleared her eyes of resentment a few minutes ago, found them brimming with tears of mirth. There was no one else like Lawrence Leighton she thought: part Puck, part Hamlet, part Merlin. He was bigger than life, some magical, elemental character out of mythology. His temper was mercurial and could plunge from exhaltation to despair in a matter of minutes. He was fascinating and bewildering. And he used people up, burned them out with his intensity and drive. Then, when they disintegrated, he was hurt and bewildered, like a child who has broken a favorite toy.

Even now, when she no longer felt the way she once had, Catriona was aware of the mesmerizing pull of his quicksilver personality and the rampant electricity of his physical appeal. She put a little more distance between them. She had broken away from him to save her identity, to keep from shriveling into a mere appendage of Lawrence Leighton. It had been as painful as radical surgery, but necessary to her very survival. He had never really understood why she had had to go, and now he apparently thought they could pick up the pieces and start where they'd left off. He still didn't understand.

"Are you ready?" he asked, smiling but impatient.

Cat's face sobered. "I can't go, Lawrence." But she stopped. There was no use going into explanations with him. "Thank you, anyway." She smiled and was relieved to realize that she meant it.

"But I've chartered a plane!"

"No, Lawrence." She tiptoed up and planted a sisterly kiss on his cheek. "Good-bye." A patron, recognizing Lawrence, came up to congratulate him on his latest best-seller.

Cat took the opportunity to make a graceful retreat, but as she did so, Adam Hawk looked up and his blue eyes met hers speculatively. She could feel her cheeks burning as she crossed the room. Dammit, why didn't he leave her alone?

She managed her escape without further incident and walked to the parking lot with a sigh of relief. It was a beautiful June evening, unusually warm, and the late sunset of a Michigan summer was still an hour away. As she unlocked the car, the breeze from the river tugged at her hair and carried the distant sound of a freighter to her ears. It would be good to get home and relax.

But when she arrived at the big brick house in Palmer Park that Angelica had inherited from her parents, Cat found she was too keyed-up from her encounters with Lawrence and Adam Hawk to relax at all. Not even a long soak in the tub with a glass of white wine did anything to soothe her edginess. Once in bed, she tried to read but was unable to concentrate, so she lay in the darkened room, watching the shadows of the lilac tree dance across the ceiling in the moonlight until Angelica came in shortly after midnight.

Cat dozed then, dream images flitting through her mind until one face, one person became dominant. Adam Hawk. She saw his proud, handsome face with the fine, high cheekbones, and those blue eyes that seemed to penetrate her heart. She saw the thin aquiline nose with chiseled nostrils, the lips that twisted cynically or parted in a wide smile. Lips that had touched her hand so softly . . .

The pained cry of an ambulance woke her, and Cat lay alone in her own bed with the night sounds of the city floating in her open windows. Damn Adam Hawk! He'd come uninvited to her jewelry showing and now had come unbidden into her dreams.

She tossed and turned, but it was a long time before sleep came again. Everytime she seemed on the verge of dropping off, Hawk intruded. Her artist's eye remembered the line and shape of his lean body. She knew how he would look with his shirt off, his chest broad, his shoulders strong and arms sinewed, the musculature well-defined. And those arms would be strong and warm around her, his lips would come down on hers, softly at first, tender, and then more demanding . . .

She fell asleep, dreaming that she lay safe in the circle of his arms.

Catriona woke to the morning sun and the smell of coffee.

"Wake up, sleepyhead! You have to be at the gallery in an hour."

Cat groaned and opened one eye. Angelica was dressed and looked ready to conquer the world, her long honey-blond hair coiled and knotted in a chic style that suited her elegant features.

"How can anyone be so damned cheerful in the morning," Cat complained, pulling the covers over her head.

"That's no way to talk to someone bearing a cup of hot coffee. And the morning paper with the review of your exhibition—"

Cat sat up, instantly more alert, and grabbed the

newspaper. There it was, Page 1C of the *Detroit Free Press*, the critique of her first major show. She pushed back the curl of burnished red hair that fell over her cheek and scanned the article.

"Strength and Beauty in Local Artist's Exhibit," the caption read. A photo of the gold-veined silver leaf necklace ran below. "Remember the name Catriona Frazer," the write-up began. "Although once you've seen her work, it will be impossible to forget . . ." Cat read rapidly: "unique" and "a rhapsody in gold, silver, and beautifully set stones" were two of the glowing phrases that her eye as she searched for negative comments. There were none.

Well, so much for Adam Hawk, she thought. She hoped he was also reading the review right now, and just wished she could see his face.

"What are you looking so fierce about?" Angelica asked. "It's a terrific review."

"Adam Hawk! He didn't like my work. And he wasn't very tactful about it, either. I'd like to take this newspaper and rub his nose in it."

"I wouldn't want to try it." Angelica laughed. "But I'm surprised you'd say that, because he said a lot of very nice things about you last night at the gallery."

Instantly Cat felt surprise mixed with curiosity, and there was an odd sinking sensation in the pit of her stomach. "A new conquest, Angel?" She had to ask the question.

"Are you kidding? I batted my eyelashes and flashed him my best smile, but all he wanted to do was talk about *you*. He said you were really good, that you'd be one of the best if you could get back in touch with your deeper emotions." Angelica smiled, delighted to be the bearer of compliments from the man whose work her friend had long admired. "And he said he wanted to offer you a job working with him."

"*Damn* him," Cat exclaimed, jumping out of bed. "Who does he think he is? I'll show him!" She headed into the bathroom, shutting the door firmly. She immediately opened it again and peeked around the threshold.

"What kind of a job?" Her voice sounded artificially casual to her own ears.

"I don't know. I gathered you'd be able to work at your jewelry full-time and make a living at it too."

Cat's heart leaped, and she felt the excitement she had been too angry to feel the night before. To be able to quit her part-time job as a restorer and spend all her time doing the work she loved! But to work with Adam Hawk? Her face clouded. She sensed that working closely with him would pose a danger to her shaky, newfound independence. He was too strong, too forceful, too overpowering. She walked back to the bed and picked up the newspaper with its glowing review and frowned at it.

"Boy, do you look grumpy." Angelica laughed. "If this is what a hint of success does to you, I'd hate to be around when you're rich and famous."

Cat smiled and threw a pillow at her. She *was* irritable, and it was all the fault of that arrogant Indian. This should have been her moment of triumph, but he had spoiled it with his blunt words, which somehow far outweighed all the praise she'd received in the press. "Angel, you know I'm always a grump in the morning. There's something about cheery sunshine and birds singing that makes me want to burrow back under the covers."

"Well, listen, I have to get down to the City County building before I lose my job. Congratulations, again!"

After Angelica left, Cat showered and put on a blue silk dress that brought out deep copper highlights in her hair and made her skin glow like ivory. She was rummaging through her purse for some blusher and lip gloss when her hand touched Hawk's handkerchief, still wrapped around the Narcissus mirror she'd made. She pulled the scarf out and his card fell out onto the dresser top.

Cat ignored the card, but she took out the small silver octagonal mirror. Lovingly she traced the raised curves of the piece with a caressing finger, as if it were the face of someone she loved. The look and feel of it flooded her with pleasure and pride.

Cat felt something on her cheek and brushed at it. She saw it was a tear and stared at it uncomprehendingly for a moment. Then she was crying, softly at first and then aloud, her breath coming in great ragged gasps. She flung herself down on the bed and cried her heart out until the emotional storm was over.

There was no need to search deeply for her tears: for months, a terrible fear had been growing in her. A fear that somewhere along the line she had taken a wrong turn and that her work, which meant everything to Cat, had lost the vital spark that gave it life. Hawk's words came back to haunt her. "A good design. Precise workmanship . . . nothing more . . ."

She had fooled the critics, but there was no way she could fool an artist of Adam Hawk's caliber. He had seen beneath the technical perfection and knew her secret. And she couldn't fool herself any longer, either.

Then she remembered something else he'd said when she'd been too hurt and angry to assimilate it. Hawk had said he could help her. Would he be able to help her regain the vitality and joy that was in her earlier work? It didn't seem likely, and yet he had seemed so sure.

And that vague mention of a job, was that part of it? Despite the harsh interpretation she had placed on his words to her, Hawk had been complimentary regarding her work, at least according to Angelica's comments. And the silver mirror, the fact that he'd come to see her exhibit, showed more than a casual interest in her work.

She rolled over and stared at the ceiling. There was really no choice. She had to do it. Clutching the Narcissus mirror like a talisman, Cat looked up the number of his hotel in the phone book. Then she took a deep breath and dialed.

Chapter Three

When she walked through the heavy glass doors of the Walker Gallery, Catriona was still unsettled. She'd been unable to get through to Adam Hawk by phone, and she felt as if her future were up in the air. She'd left a message at the hotel asking him to call her at the gallery. Now that she'd made up her mind, now that she'd accepted his criticisms as valid, she was terribly anxious to talk to him.

As she crossed the deep, snowy carpeting, Mabel Walker approached, her fashionably streaked blond hair pulled back in a French twist and her round figure expensively clothed in a suit of beige linen. "Catriona, my dear child! Did you see the review in this morning's *Free Press*? And someone from the *News* just called and wants to interview you for their Sunday magazine. You should be terribly gratified by the response." Mabel chatted on, oblivious to Cat's subdued yet restless air. "That sapphire-blue dress is perfect with your coloring." Mabel reached out to touch the soft waves of fiery hair that curled around Cat's shoulders. "It looks beautiful down. Such a lovely shade, and not at all carroty. Is it real? It is? What a shame! I was thinking of having mine tinted the same color, but I suppose Henri would never be able to duplicate it." Her voice trailed off regretfully. "Oh, and Bonnie had a message for you."

Grateful to escape the deluge of words, Cat thanked Mabel and headed for the office. Mabel was a kindhearted and intelligent woman, but as Cat's father would have said, her tongue "ran on wheels."

She found Bonnie Ross, Mabel's second-in-command, behind the graceful Queen Anne desk, opening the morning mail. Cat loved the office with its elegant Chippendale love seats flanking the marble fireplace. And Bonnie, with her cap of close cropped curls framing her beautifully sculpted brown face, fit in perfectly.

"Congratulations, Cat! How does it feel to be a smashing success?" She smiled warmly. "Goodness knows you deserve it."

"Thanks, Bonnie. Mabel said you had a message for me?"

"Really *two* messages. I just took a call from a certain lady associated with one of the old-line families. She wants to buy your necklace, the one with the gold and silver leaves."

"Oh, that's terrific!" All thoughts of her problems and of Adam Hawk were driven from Cat's mind by the happy news. "I was afraid with the price of gold no one would want to pay out that kind of money. But, you know, it's sad, too. Between the expense of the gold and having to tie my money up in a piece that may not sell for months or years, that necklace might well be my last major piece in gold."

"Your other message is here somewhere." Bonnie shuffled through the papers with thin, capable hands. "Ah, here it is. Adam Hawk returned your call while you were on your way to the gallery. You just missed him. He said he'll be out all afternoon, but he'll be by to pick you up here for dinner at seven-thirty."

Cat's brows rose in annoyance. She wanted to talk with him, not dine with him! He was as bad as Lawrence, assuming he could run other people's lives for them. Then she grinned. Even Hawk couldn't be as pushy and dominating as Lawrence, who was the master of the art.

"Thanks, Bonnie." Cat returned to the showrooms in a lighter frame of mind, greeting guests and answering the questions of a reporter with aplomb. While she tried to give all her attention to the business at hand, her mind kept sprinting forward in time. She found that she could hardly wait for seven-thirty to come.

As they approached the RenCen, the mirrored towers glittered in the early-June sunshine like giant candles, reflecting the bright rays back in a challenge to the sky. Hart Plaza was already crowded with people celebrating the first day of the Irish Festival, and the sunken amphitheater was thronged. Sounds of a lovely ballad drifted on the breeze, and the river sparkled in the background as energetic sailboats and tugs darted around a Russian freighter silhouetted against the opposite Canadian shore.

"I didn't expect Detroit to look like this," Hawk said.

"What did you picture?" Cat asked.

"Oh, empty storefronts and lots of factories, nobody moving around downtown. Sort of an industrial ghost town." He laughed at himself.

"Well, every big city had its problems, but things are turning around. I'll have to take you to Trapper's Alley and the Bricktown area while you're here." They talked about pleasant trivialities as they went through the multistoried hotel lobby to the bank of elevators, but as they rode up, a silence fell over them. When the doors opened, they revealed not the restaurant, but a floor of hotel rooms. Cat stopped short and Hawk took her by the elbow and propelled her down the hall to the second door.

As he unlocked the door, Hawk looked down at her and unsuccessfully tried to hide a smile. "Acquit me of any ulterior motives," he said with amusement in his voice. "I knew we would want to talk privately, so I ordered dinner to be served here." The room was done in soothing shades of sand and rust accented with vibrant blues. The soft light filtering through the sheer curtains lent an air of intimacy to the scene. She walked across the thick carpet to the wall of glass that overlooked the bustling river traffic far below. The sun, although lowering on the western horizon, would still be shining for another two hours.

"It stays light a long time at this latitude," Adam said from close behind her, and Cat jumped. She hadn't heard him follow her. Then she felt the movement of his breath on her hair, and his nearness sent shivers down her spine. Confused by the effect he had on her, Cat tried to move away, but she only succeeded in colliding with his broad chest.

Hawk's hand came up to grasp her shoulders and steady her, and for a brief instant her breasts made contact with his chest. A shock wave of response ran along her nerves, and the sudden pressure of his body against hers told Cat that he was not as unaffected as he appeared. He took in a sharp breath and his eyes searched her face. Then he bent his head as if to kiss her, but the fright Cat felt must have been evident on her face.

With an effort he lifted his head, and his hands fell to his sides. Cat moved away a little and he kept his distance, watching her warily, as if afraid she might suddenly bolt and run.

"Cat . . ." he began softly, but a discreet knock heralded the arrival of the waiter with their dinner. Adam seated Catriona and there was no further conversation until they were alone.

"Tell me," she said between mouthfuls of chicken stuffed with mushrooms and provolone, "what's this job offer about?"

He answered her obliquely at first. "There are few things in life as rewarding as knowing that some principle or skill will be handed down to others because of something you've said or done. And every artist has the obligation to pass his or her special vision to those who are eager to learn." As he spoke, his eyes took on a special glow and he seemed to be looking at a distant horizon. Cat felt an echoing thrill along her nerves. To influence the future! To leave her mark on the world by training others to follow in her footsteps. Some of the fervor in Hawk's face was reflected in hers.

Adam scowled then. "You've probably seen some of the shoddy imitation Indian jewelry being sold. And I don't mean just the inexpensive stuff."

Cat nodded. "Some of it's atrocious. I saw a squash-blossom necklace that must have had four pounds of silver in it. Big, with a price tag to match. I wanted to melt it down, it was so ugly and poorly done, but I didn't think the woman wearing it would have appreciated the gesture."

"Yes. I know the type of jewelry you mean," Adam answered. "Well, did you know that some of it's made by Indians?" His voice was quiet, filled with bitterness, and Cat was startled both by the information and his tone.

"No, I didn't."

"Some of them are tired of poverty. Others just don't care. They say that silverwork is just something they learned from the Spanish conquerors and not 'real' Indian tradition. They just knock out those shabby imitations one after another, and unfortunately people buy them and pay a stiff price, too!"

"Where do I come into the picture?" Cat asked. "Why did you come to Detroit looking for me?" His eyes held hers and she knew that what he had to say was very important to him.

"I've started a training school, not just for Indians, but for the others who share my vision. I need you to help me teach them." The sunlight coming through the curtained glass warmed his fine, high cheekbones and shadowed the hollows below in sharp relief. "The tribal council has come around and provided the land. We use an old government building for the various workshops. In time we'll add dormitories and other things as the need arises. My goal is to build as much of a self-supporting community as possible. We would raise our own food, and the apprentices would be there on a sort of scholarship, so they wouldn't have to pay for the training. We already have a small flock of sheep.

"There's a master weaver and a journeyman silversmith so far—that's almost enough to start out with but I want to do something special. I can teach them the old ways of working with metal and stones, the traditional patterns, and how to put their spirit into every piece they craft. I am the best at that." He said the last words simply, a statement of fact with no conceit or false modesty, and Cat was impressed by his honesty and detached appraisal. He *was* the best, and she knew it too.

She sat patiently, knowing the rest of the story would be forthcoming. He stared down at his hands, turning them over as if seeing them for the first time. Then he looked back at her and his face was a mixture of emotions that puzzled her, as doubt, hope, and eagerness flitted over his face. And something that almost appeared to be despair. But it was gone in a flash, leaving her unsure of what she had seen. Her perplexity must have registered on her face because Hawk took in a quick breath and went on.

"I need you. I need someone with your unexpected vision, someone who can take the ordinary materials and turn them into something extraordinary, as you did with the mirror. Following tradition *only* will leave the students stunted as artists. Their work would be stale and boring.

"As the school's director, I can offer you room and board, and a small stipend. And materials, of course. And I think I can help you bring your 'spirit' into your work again." He sat back as if waiting for her judgment.

Catriona looked out at the wake of a freighter passing far below, and its sad call sounded distantly. She suddenly identified with the ship making its way through the currents of the Detroit River. She'd been alone, trying to find her way in unfamiliar waters, crying out her loneliness and wondering if there were anyone out there to hear her voice. She'd longed for the companionship of other artists, longed to have the freedom to devote her time to her life's work. She knew that Hawk was right about her obligation to pass her vision and skills to young artists eager to learn from her. And if things didn't work out, she'd always have the money from the sale of the gold leaf necklace to fall back on.

"What about the remarks you made last night at my exhibit? How can you ask me to work with your apprentices when you don't *like* my work?"

"I said that you were good, but that you could be the *best*. That you *should* be the best. There's fine craftmanship and a tremendous understanding of your materials in every line. The only thing missing is that spark, that certain essence that turns something good into something *great*. You still have that spark in you: your ring shows it." He was standing then, grasping her hands and pulling her to her feet. Catriona found herself caught up in his enthusiasm and in his belief in her. The sun came streaming through the window as a bank of fleecy clouds shifted, illuminating them like a spotlight, turning her hair to a radiant aureole.

She wasn't sure what she wanted to do. No, that was wrong. She knew. She wanted to go with Adam Hawk and work with him and his apprentices. She wanted to go with Adam Hawk *anywhere*. A flood of consternation went through her. He was a man whose work she had long admired, and now he was a man who had stirred her blood like no one since her romance with Lawrence. Or even before. He was dynamically masculine and vital, and she was suddenly afraid.

As if he'd seen her wavering emotions, Adam spoke again. "One year," he said. "And a contract, renewable for five years after the first, if you want it. But during the first year, you can walk out anytime you decide you want to leave." He paused for a moment. "Life on the reservation will be a challenge for you."

Cat searched his face as if to find the answer there. "You've told me the what and the where, but not the *why*."

Hawk reached into his pocket and pulled something out. It glittered like moonlight against the velvet cloth in which he held it, and Cat was speechless in surprise. It was a necklace she'd designed two summers ago, and it had been sold to an unknown Chicago buyer.

"This is why," he said almost fiercely. "I was struck by the way you used the moonstones." He fingered one of the milky ovals of translucent feldspar that were sunken below the wide silver band of the neck collar and were revealed through holes cut into the top surface. "And I thought your use of the braided silver wire on the hammered silver background was unique and innovative." The moonstones and metal pieces seemed luminous against his deeply bronzed hand. "But most of all," he went on with a strange half-smile, "I felt when I touched it that the artist was someone I wanted to know." He held the piece of jewelry out to her. "This," he said softly, "and the Narcissus mirror are what brought me to Detroit. And that's why I was disappointed by the things I saw in your show yesterday."

Catriona picked up the necklace and blinked away the sting of tears that brightened her dark-lashed eyes. She knew that he was right. The piece she held in her hand was one of her earlier works, and while it was perhaps not as perfectly wrought as the items in the exhibit that had won her several prizes and much praise, she had to acknowledge its superiority. She replaced the necklace and bowed her head on her graceful neck.

"I've lost it," she said. She pushed back her chair

and started to rise. "I had it once, but I've lost it. And you're the only one who has seen it, besides me." She raised a hand to shield her eyes so he wouldn't see the tears, but he was already on his feet and grasping her shoulders before she had even seen him move. The man was like a panther, she thought, startled by his quick, silent agility.

"No, Catriona," he said, using her full given name to address her for the first time since they'd met. "Your ring shows you haven't lost that passion, that special gift of translating your emotions into your work." He lifted her chin so that she had to look up at him, and his blue eyes sparkled. He moved his hand along her jawline, cradled her cheek against his palm, and then traced a line of excitement from her temple down to the corner of her mouth.

Cat felt her lips tremble, saw his gaze drop from her eyes to her mouth and back again. He pulled her against his hard length and she felt her bones melt with the warmth that radiated from his body to hers. Her breath came more quickly and he slid his hand behind her head, tangling his long fingers in the wealth of her silky red hair. Her lips parted slightly and his breath was uneven. She saw his eyes light with naked desire.

He pulled her more tightly against him and she felt as if she couldn't breathe, but she didn't care. There was nothing in her mind, nothing in her world but this man who had only a moment ago seemed so civilized, but now looked at her with such primitive and savage longing that she was caught up in his vortex of passion. As her eyes closed, his mouth came down on hers, demanding all she had to give. His hands moved up and down her back, holding her body against his and molding their contours together. Then he smoothed the roundness of her hips and brought them against his, so that she had no doubt of his urgent need.

His tongue invaded her mouth, touching, tasting. A surge of desire flamed through her veins like a raging brushfire, igniting every nerve in her anatomy. Catriona found her body pressing against his with a hungry insistence of its own as he then kissed her eyelids, her temple, the curve of her white throat. He held her close in his iron embrace as one of his hands sought her breast, caressing it through the silk fabric of her dress. Cat moaned low in her throat.

The soft sound she made seemed to inflame him more. His hand moved to the buttons at the top of her dress. His warm lips followed his fingers and he kissed the curve of her breast above the lace of her bra.

She arched her back to his seeking mouth and he kissed her throat, then buried his face in the fragrant cloud of her hair. She moved to his rhythm and they kissed deeply, hungrily, and his strong fingers unfastened the buttons to her waist. He moved his hands over her bare flesh, around to her back, fumbling to undo the tiny hooks that held her bra in place. His knee moved between her legs, urging them apart.

One instant Cat was caught up in his fever of

excitement and the next she was panicked and frightened. Things were out of control, moving way too fast. She felt as if she were losing herself, as if she were being consumed by the heat of their mutual passion.

She struggled against him and Adam stopped instantly, his face still flushed with arousal. His eyes raked her face as he continued to hold her captive in his embrace.

"I'm sorry," she gasped. "I didn't mean—" She stopped, suddenly embarrassed and angry with both herself and him.

"Cat," he said softly, but she pulled away and straightened her dress, quickly buttoning the buttons he'd just undone.

"I'd better go," she said, glancing wildly around the room for her purse.

"Look," he said a little shakily. "I never intended for that to happen. God! You went to my head like wine! It's been a long time since I reacted like that to a woman." He was talking quickly, trying to explain things before she fled the room. "I . . . the school needs you, Catriona Frazer. And there's no stipulation that you have to sleep with the director."

Cat stopped short and stared at him. She saw him compose his proud face into an aloof expression, but she knew he was as aware as she was of the strong current of attraction that still flowed between them. The memory of the abandoned response they had just shared filled the room. And yet she didn't leave.

"When do you need a decision?" she asked softly.

"Now."

"So soon?" Cat responded with astonishment.

"I'll be going back next weekend. Come with me, Cat." As he spoke, she thought she saw a fleeting look of sadness cross his features. She had an incredible urge to reach out her hand and touch his cheek. And as she gazed at him she realized that, despite her hammering heart and her repressed sense of panic she really had no choice.

"When do we leave?"

Chapter Four

They were winging their way through clear azure skies, and Catriona felt her excitement growing as they drew nearer to Flagstaff and the end of the first leg of their journey. The past few days had been a blur of frantic activity, but now she could finally sit back and draw a deep breath. At least for a while. Luckily she had no lease to worry about, since she had lived in Angelica's house for a nominal rent. "Just for the company," Angelica had told Cat when she first moved in. Angelica, however, was as enthusiastic about the school as Cat was herself, and she had actively encouraged Cat's decision to go to Arizona with Hawk.

"Don't worry," Angelica had exclaimed. "Just go and have a marvelous adventure! I can always get another roommate if you decide to stay in Arizona."

Cat sipped her chilled glass of wine as she watched the land far below. The landscape they passed over was red and ocher and dun, a world completely different from the green and gold patterns of the fertile Great Plains and the lake-dotted scenery of the Midwest.

"We'll be landing shortly," Adam said, his voice a low counterpoint to the rumble of the jet's engines.

She turned to see that he had put away the portfolio of papers he'd been working on. "Any last-minute qualms about leaving civilization behind and coming out to the reservation with me?"

She could tell by his voice that he was concerned. "Not since we've agreed to keep our relationship purely professional," she answered.

His jaw muscles tensed and he sat still for a moment before answering. "Despite your many charms and the episode between us the other evening, I think you can trust me to control myself," he said stiffly. "I've never been one to force my attentions on women." His face was as cold and hard as his words.

Cat flushed. "I didn't mean that as a reflection on you, Adam," she tried to explain. "I told you earlier, it's my own problem. We're both aware of the attraction between us, but I'm not ready to handle any kind of relationship right now."

The stern look remained on his face for a few seconds before his expression softened. "I'm sorry," he said in a soft voice that did strange things to the pit of her stomach. Just as his passionate actions roused passionate reactions in her, so too his tenderness softened her mood. Cat knew she was going to have her work cut out for her just trying to keep her own part of the agreement she'd insisted on making with him. But she was determined; their relationship would have to be strictly business. Her ego wasn't strong enough to take another chance at romance yet, and she was determined not to be hurt again.

"Tell me more about the school and Peshlakai,"

she said to take her mind off his nearness. He had told her about the small settlement that had grown up around the school, and that Peshlakai meant "silver" or "silversmith." She thought it a good name and, hopefully, a good omen.

Adam continued to describe their destination. "As I said, the buildings aren't much. The school itself is an old adobe government building we've renovated. We'd like to get running water inside, but that's something that's very scarce on the reservation.

"Oh?" Cat said. She wondered what other surprises there were in store for her in the immediate future. "Ah, what kind of facilities do you have there now?"

"We have water piped into the kitchen from a storage container, although it has to be heated on the stove. And there's an outdoor shower."

"And little buildings with half-moons on the doors?"

"Something like that," he admitted with a rueful grin. "But probably not as fancy as what you have in mind." Despite the laughter in his eyes, he was watching her reactions carefully.

She took a swallow of her wine. "Does this mean I have to chop firewood and keep a few chickens on the side?"

Adam laughed and took her left hand in one of his. "No, not with these hands," he told her. "These are an artist's hands and should be treated like the priceless treasures they are." He laid his other hand over hers and a warm tingle shivered up her arm and down her back. She wondered if Adam realized how much of a threat he was to her shaky determinations. She certainly hoped not.

"But," he added, still holding her hand in his, "if you want to help out occasionally with the lighter tasks, that's all right. Just remember than you're an instructor, not a laborer." He looked down then and saw her hand still in his as if he had not noticed it before. He slowly released her.

She took his words at face value. She would only serve the school's purpose if she could fulfill her teaching obligations. "While we're on the subject," she said. "Do you have any more . . . ah, little secrets you've kept from me?"

Adam looked startled for a moment. "Not that I can think of," he said finally. Just then the flight attendant came down the aisle and picked up the trays of an unidentifiable substance masquerading as beef bourguignon. Cat relinquished her untouched portion without regret.

"I'd like to know more about the people I'll be working with," she said to Adam.

"Joseph Osborne, who will be your only apprentice to start, has a lot of potential. There's a problem with his attitude, though, and I'm afraid it may be his undoing. He wants to start at the top, and he wants to make a lot of money right away. I'm afraid he's in for a lot of disappointment."

"And Ben Slowhorse is the other journeyman silversmith?"

"Yes. He has a true love for his silverwork and it shows in everything he does. He is . . . But I'll let you see for yourself. You'll like Ben. Ben will welcome you." Adam was silent for a moment.

Cat wondered about his last statement. The way he had said. "Ben will welcome you," made her wonder if the others wouldn't. Well, she'd know soon enough.

"There must be other women at the school?" she prompted at last when the silence stretched out uncomfortably.

"Yes. Smiling Woman, the wife of Donald Chen, is our master weaver. She has both the traditional Navaho loom and a modern setup to teach other techniques. She is the mother of Lee Chen, one of the weaving apprentices."

"Chen doesn't sound like a Navaho name," Cat commented.

"It's not. Donald Chen is of Chinese descent. Many Chinese people settled in the Old West, and their children's children remain there. He is a social worker among The Dinee."

Cat had picked up a book on Navaho culture at the RenCen bookstore, and now she remembered that the Navaho refer to themselves as The Dinee, which literally means The People. And to The People, all the rest of the world are outsiders. The Enemy People.

Suddenly Cat's bright sense of adventure seemed tarnished. She wondered just what she was doing, going off to a different culture with a completely different philosophy and life-style. Cat wondered how she would deal with being an outsider. It was not a comforting thought.

"Ben, Joseph, and Lee all speak excellent English, and Maria Tso, who does the cooking and cleaning for us, does quite well when she wants to," Adam commented, but if he thought this tidbit would cheer Cat up, he was sadly mistaken. It had never occurred to her that people on the reservation would still speak the Navaho tongue, and she mentally berated her naïveté. Her doubts were growing stronger by the minute.

"Passengers, please note that the captain has turned on the fasten-seat-belt sign," a disembodied voice announced over the intercom. Suddenly all Cat's fears were washed away in the rush of excitement that filled her. She looked out the window, but saw only scattered wastes of brown and gray on her side of the plane. When she turned back, Adam was watching her intently.

"What's wrong?" she asked.

"Nothing. I was just thinking that you look like a camellia . . . or a rose, with your delicate coloring. And I was wondering if such a dainty blossom will be able to survive in the heat and harshness of the high country." He looked at her, a strange light in his blue eyes as they held hers. "I'm like a cactus, you know. I can survive anything that life has to offer without much damage. I just sink my roots down more deeply and bide my time."

She met his gaze levelly. "You're forgetting my hardy Scottish heritage. I think I'm really more like a kind of heather—I look fragile, but I'm much tougher than you'd think at first sight."

The corners of Adam's mouth quirked up. "Yes,"

he replied with a slow smile. "The lovely purple heather that looks so dry and dead, and then bursts into life with the first kiss of spring." His gaze traveled from her eyes to her lips and lingered there a moment.

Cat felt as if he'd touched them with his own, felt the remembered warmth of his mouth on hers. She had an incredible urge to tell him to forget their "bargain," but she struggled successfully against it. Later, perhaps, when she knew just who she was and where she intended to go with her life. With an unconscious sigh of regret, she looked away.

The plane began its curving descent into Flagstaff, and Cat caught a glimpse of the dark peak of Mount Humphreys in the distance, its flanks covered with the first green trees she had seen since Iowa. The plane landed smoothly, but before the mighty roar of the reversing engines drowned out all other sound, Adam reached out his hand and touched her arm. When he spoke, his words had the cadence of a prayer or chant.

"Welcome, Heather Woman, to the land of The People. May you always walk in beauty."

They picked up Adam's Blazer from the airport lot and Cat looked around eagerly as they headed through town. This fascinating land, with its rich heritage of artistry and design, was her new home, and she knew her work would be profoundly influenced by it.

"I have to make a stop here," Adam said, pulling

into a small shopping center around a cobbled court. "Come inside and meet my friends."

The interior of the building was cool, with whitewashed walls and fine examples of Santa Clara pottery gleaming like ebony on lighted glass shelves. A rectangle of glass counters filled the center of the shop, and a handsome woman of Spanish ancestry stood behind them, polishing a wide cuff bracelet of inlaid silver.

"Silversinger!" she exclaimed when she saw them enter. "It's good to see you again." She eyed Cat with interest. "And this is your new silversmith for Peshlakai?" She held out a slim olive hand decked in many rings, and Cat took it in hers.

"This is Carla Marshall, Cat. Carla owns this shop and another in Sedona, and she handles a lot of our work from Peshlakai.

While Adam and Carla talked business for a while, Cat roamed the store, admiring the lovely items. "Silversinger," Carla had called Adam. Cat decided it must be a nickname. She asked Adam about when they resumed their journey, and he laughed.

"You'll find that I have many names among The People—and so, in time, will you. In Anglo society, only criminals, actors, and writers have pseudonyms, but in our culture a person has many names in addition to the secret 'war name' given them at birth. On the reservation I am Silversinger and Adam Hawk and Adam Longshadow, and a host of other less flattering names."

"Anything else I should know?"

"Well, I should probably warn you about something." Adam's face was serious, but she saw a smile hovering around the edges of his mouth.

"I'm almost afraid to ask," she said with a sidelong glance from under her lashes.

"Oh, it's just that the Navaho are rather famous for their practical jokes and intricate puns. When you pick up some of the language, you'll have to be very careful or you'll say the wrong thing. Or worse yet, you'll say the right word and it will have three or four different meanings, and everyone in earshot will chose to interpret it in the wrong way."

"Oh, great! Outhouses, a language I'll never be able to understand unless I want to make enemies, and a bunch of inveterate jokers! Is this all in my contract?"

Adam turned toward her with a wide smile. "Of course." They drove on in companionable silence, and after a while Cat watched him instead of the scenery. His profile was handsome, the aristocratic nose long and thin, the chin strong, the forehead high and smooth.

His hands were well-shaped and had a look of strength about them. They were well-kept, but she noticed the callus ridges that crossed each palm in a diagonal line from wrist to ring finger. Cat knew they weren't from silvermaking, and she wondered if they were from riding horseback and holding the reins. He'd said earlier that he had several horses.

He held the wheel like a lover, she thought, noticing the way his hands caressed it, his touch light yet sure. Instantly she was embarrassed by her mental image, but there was something so elementally masculine about him that he made her constantly aware that she was a woman. Adam turned slightly, catching the expression on her face.

"Don't look at me like that, Heather Woman," he said softly. "Or I might not be able to keep my promise." One of his fingers reached over and stroked her cheek. A jolt of electricity shot through her, and her heart pounded erratically.

Suddenly a red pickup cut them off. Adam swore and swerved the Blazer into the next lane to avoid a collision. The near accident should have broken the air of intimacy between them, but the tension grew moment by moment as they rode on.

Cat stared out the window at the dun countryside dotted with round juniper bushes and unfamiliar plants. She was trying to ignore her thoughts, but they kept circling back to one burning speculation: if a light and casual caress filled her whole body with wild sensations, what would it be like to spend a night in Adam Hawk's arms? She was in over her head, and she knew it.

They had at least two hours before they would reach Peshlakai, Adam told her, and Cat began to find the scenery barren and monotonous. After a while she leaned her head back, just to close her eyes for a few minutes.

The next thing she knew, Adam was shaking her gently. "Wake up, Cat. I want to show you something." She opened her eyes and saw that they were driving up the side of a sandy hill. The countryside seemed otherwise unchanged, until they reached the summit. They were on a fairly level surface, and blocks of fallen limestone and pieces of sandstone were strewn by nature along the left side, like remnants of some great wall. Other than that, there didn't seem to be much to see.

While Cat rubbed the sleep from her eyes, Adam came around and opened the door. He helped her out of the Blazer and led her past the pile of tumbled rock.

She couldn't believe her eyes. Spread out below them and reaching to the distant horizon was a land filled with red and orange rock formations that the wind and weather had carved into a hundred strange shapes. Twisted spires, sheer needles that pierced the sky, flat mesas, and curtains of stone lay scattered along the plain. She recognized it as the famous Monument Valley from a hundred magazines and brochures. The alien beauty of the scene had a powerful impact on Cat. She turned to Adam, her eyes shining.

"It's breathtaking. I've never seen anything like it."

"There is nothing like it," he answered. His face glowed with pride and his joy in homecoming. This, Cat thought, is Adam's country. This, in all the world, is where he belongs.

Adam looked down at her now, and there was something in his eyes that made her catch her breath. Without thinking, her hand went up to touch his face. She took a step closer, moving as though hypnotized, and her breasts brushed against his chest. Instantly, one of his long hands slid behind her head, cradling it as he tangled his fingers in her hair. He pulled her hard against him and his lips came down on hers hungrily. He kissed her once, and then, with their own will, her arms wound around his neck.

Adam's lips moved warmly across her cheek and down the tender column of her throat as he murmured soft words against her skin. She slid her hands over the taut muscles of his arms and shoulders, delighting in the feel of his hard supple body, totally lost in the sensations he was arousing in her as his hand sought and found her straining breasts. She gasped, and then his mouth was back on hers, nibbling, tasting. Urgent flames of desire lapped at her, spreading through her body until they threatened to engulf her.

Cat's heart beat wildly as the touch of Adam's mouth and hands evoked thoughts and images she was unable to control. She wished that they were not out in the open with the wind and hot sun, but in some cool, dim room, lying naked in each other's arms as they quenched the fires of their passion.

Adam's kisses grew more urgent. His tongue parted her lips, invading her mouth as their kiss deepened. Yet even while Cat abandoned herself to the moment, even while her body craved more, a distant part of her mind protested. Too soon, too soon! She ignored her inner promptings as Adam's hands moved over her body, slipping inside her blouse to tantalize the tips of her bare breasts until she was dizzy with longing. His fingers circled the full peaks and his body pressed against hers until they were molded tightly together.

Unexpectedly it was Adam who broke the spell that held them both. He lifted his mouth from hers, his eyes dazed like those of a sleepwalker, and held her away from him.

"Ah, Wild Heather Woman. You make it hard for a man to keep his promises," he whispered in a deep and ragged voice. He put his hands on either side of her face, bent his head, and kissed her roughly. "Let this be your warning. I won't be so noble the next time." Abruptly he let go of her and walked over to the car without a backward glance.

Cat was in a state of shock. She quickly straightened her blouse, trying to appear calmer than she felt. Her emotions were all roiled and the needs that he had aroused in her unsatisfied. No man had ever walked away from her like that before. She was hurt and angry and felt demeaned in a way she couldn't explain.

As she slowly walked back to the Blazer, the angry flush on her cheeks changed to one of mortification. *She* had been the one to insist that there be nothing between them but a professional relationship. And now she had been the first one to break that rule. She got back into the vehicle. Adam stared straight ahead through the windshield, his face cool and unreadable. As she shut the door, he turned the key in the ignition.

"Whenever you're ready," he said.

Cat didn't know if he was refering to the rest of their journey, or to something else altogether. She didn't dare to ask for clarification.

Chapter Five

"How much farther to the reservation?" Cat asked after they had driven on for quite some time. Since leaving the weirdly beautiful rock formations of Monument Valley, they had traveled through countryside that was fairly flat and dotted with omnipresent juniper and piñon. Except for a battered pickup that had passed them much earlier, there were no signs of human habitation. It looked like a moonscape, empty and forlorn.

"We've been on it since shortly after leaving Flagstaff," Adam replied. "Monument Valley is part of the reservation. I thought you knew that."

"But where is everybody?" Cat exclaimed. "We haven't passed a single village or settlement."

"The reservation covers twenty-five thousand square miles; it's larger than all the New England states put together. The People live in small family groups here and there. We have no villages as the Hopi of Havasupai do, but when the word gets out about a ceremonial or other get-together, five or six hundred people will usually arrive at the site by evening."

Cat felt her heart sink. She'd been prepared for a

quiet, simple life, but the isolation of this land was beyond her comprehension.

Adam, however, quickly proved that he did not share her sentiments. "It's good to be back!" he said with a smile. "Sometimes I feel guilty traveling so swiftly and comfortably over such a distance, but then I wonder if my ancestors felt the same way about the horse."

"Well," Cat suggested amiably, "we could turn off the air-conditioner and stereo."

"No, thanks. The People are noted for taking the best parts of other cultures and making them their own. I could take this heat in stride." He laughed. "But I would miss the music."

It was nearly seven-thirty when they at last arrived at Peshlakai. Here, the land was more varied, and in the distance Cat could see a few bizarre shapes of red and orange sandstone rising from the flat plain. Adam turned to her, his face solemn.

"Welcome to my home, Small Heather Woman." He helped her out of the truck, and while he unloaded their baggage, Cat surveyed her new residence. There were three buildings clustered together. Two of them were traditional six-sided hogans of log-cabin-type construction, and fitted with hexagonal blue roofs. The third building, of white adobe, was long and low with a veranda stretching across the front. Cat recognized this as the actual school from Adam's description.

As Cat looked about, she saw a small-boned woman approaching from the direction of a dry wash. She wore a white cotton blouse over an ankle-length blue skirt, with a belt of oval silver conchos wound around her slim waist. The expression in her dark eyes was definitely not one of welcome.

"Maria!" Adam called out. "Come and meet Catriona."

The woman came forward gracefully and began to speak to Adam in her native tongue, pointedly ignoring Cat, who felt awkward and snubbed. Only after Adam's prodding did the Indian woman greet the new silversmith, inclining her head briefly.

"Ben is working on a necklace," Maria said. "Lee and Joseph have gone to Kayenta, but they will be back for dinner." She turned and left.

Adam looked a little embarrassed by Maria's cool reception and Cat tried to ease the situation. It was obvious to her that Maria was jealous. Cat wondered if there was some kind of relationship between Maria and Adam. She pushed the thought out of her mind. "I'm eager to meet Ben," she said. "I'd like to watch him at work, if he wouldn't mind."

"Yes, I think Ben would like that." He led Cat into the adobe building. They entered a large room furnished with a trestle table and several wooden chairs. Two old sofas covered with colorful Navaho rugs faced each other on the opposite wall, at right angles to a fireplace. There were shelves along another wall holding an assortment of pottery and books. Altogether, the room gave an impression of being plain, but cozy.

"This is our activities room—part dining room, part library, and general living quarters," Adam commented as he led her through a door on the right. They were in a small hallway, with two rooms opening off it. He went to the second door. "This is the room for metalworking."

Cat stepped over the threshold. The sun's dying rays streamed into the room through two large windows and a skylight overhead, outlining a man hunched over the long worktable on the far wall. He was as tall as Adam, but his blue-checked shirt and faded jeans bagged out from his too-thin body, and his glossy black hair, worn long in the old style of the Navaho Way, was sprinkled with silver.

Ben straightened and turned around slightly, and Cat saw that he was ancient, his dark eyes almost hidden by the heavy lids and surrounding crinkles.

"Welcome, Catriona Frazer, to the home of The People," he said in a low, musical voice. Ben extended his right hand, and when she put her own into it, his skin was dry and his touch gentle. "I know your work from Adam Silversinger, and it is good," he said.

"Thank you," she answered, pleased with his friendly reception. "Would it disturb you if I watched you work for a while?"

"It would not disturb me, but the necklace is not ready to be seen yet. Perhaps after dinner." Ben Slowhorse nodded to them and returned to his work, but Cat did not feel slighted, as she had by Maria Tso. As she turned to Adam, a piece of turquoise near Ben's elbow rolled off the worktable and fell to the wood floor. Ben looked down where the stone had first fallen, but the oblong of turquoise had rolled a foot farther.

"Behind your left boot, about an inch or so," Adam told him. Ben knelt without moving his feet, then groped without looking until he found the errant gem. He picked it up and rolled it between his fingers, feeling the stone for chips or imperfections, and it was then that the truth dawned on Cat. Ben Slowhorse, like many a silversmith before him, had succumbed to one of the hazards of the trade. He was blind.

Cat looked up at Adam, her eyes wide with shock and sympathy. He nodded confirmation, and the two of them slipped out of the room, leaving Ben to finish his work in peace.

"I was aware it happened," Cat said in a subdued voice. "But Ben is the first smith I've actually met who lost his sight."

"You know mostly younger people," Adam commented as he guided her back down the hall. "I know many who are legally blind from decades spent at their craft. Do you know what their one regret is? Not that they can't see clearly anymore, but that they cannot work silver and stones as well as they used to!"

"How much sight does he have?"

"He can see your face close up in strong light, but he can't read anymore, and that was one of his loves. He does much of his silverwork by touch and instinct. Ben still carves the molds for his pieces, but I make sure someone else pours the molten metals for him now."

Cat was quiet as Adam completed the tour. He showed her the weaving room, next door to the smith's work area, where three rugs in varying degrees of completion hung on the tall wooden looms. Cat saw a beautifully woven rug hanging on the wall next to the doorway. The weave was smooth and tight, the colors of brown and tan and sienna, soft and muted. She was compelled to go up to it and run her fingers over the soft surface.

"This is the most beautiful rug I've ever seen. Did Smiling Woman make it?" There was no answer from Adam, and she turned to look over her shoulder. He seemed carved in stone, his face grim and white lines of tension marking the corners of his mouth.

"No," he said. That was all. He stalked out the door, and Cat followed him, bewildered. She wanted to ask him to explain, but there was a harshness in his terse answer that made her hold back. She could scent a mystery and she was determined to get to the bottom of it, sooner or later.

Adam led her back across the activities room to the opposite hall. "This will be your room," he said, opening a door. The room was large, with a high, beamed ceiling, and the whitewashed walls made it seem open and airy. Two windows on the far wall framed the distant spires and buttes of the landscape, and a door led outside to the veranda. On the right was an old pine cupboard for storage and next to it sat a chair covered in soft, old leather with a matching hassock. On the left, an oversized bed covered in a brightly woven blanket stood near the adobe fireplace built into the corner of the room, and the red-tiled floor was covered with scattered rugs and a fluffy sheepskin.

"I didn't think it would be this nice after all the horror stories you told me on the plane," she chided Adam. "Did you make up the part about the outdoor privies too?"

Adam had the grace to blush. "I'm used to the way things are here, but I got wondering how it would be for someone coming in from the outside. I guess I thought if I made it sound bad enough without frightening you off, you'd be so pleasantly surprised you wouldn't mind the inconveniences that *do* exist."

"O ye of little faith! I grew up in the north woods of Michigan, with a well pump in the kitchen sink and no hot water. I told you I was made of sterner stuff! I'll do just fine here, thank you." She made a saucy face at him, and Adam grasped her chin between his strong thumb and forefinger. His dark blue eyes searched her green ones, then his lips curved up in a smile.

"Yes, Heather Woman, I think you will." He continued to look down into her eyes, and again Cat was aware of how fragile her resolves were in the presence of his profound magnetism. His thoughts seemed to be running on similar lines. He dropped his hand, as if burned, and walked over to the pine cupboard. Cat followed, keeping a safe distance between them. Every time she and Adam had the slightest physical contact she felt the electrical field generated by their attraction to one another grow stronger. And she knew he felt it too. Even now, as he showed her the linen supplies, the dark flush across his carved cheekbones betrayed him.

He showed her the tiny bathroom next door. There was no running water piped in yet, but they were building a water storage tower and would have water brought in sometime in the next year. In the meantime, bathwater was heated in huge caldrons in the kitchen, and there was a chemical toilet and an enormous water bottle suspended over the sink basin. All in all, Cat had seen worse. She could live with it.

When they reentered the activities room, Maria Tso came out of the kitchen and murmured something softly in the Navaho tongue.

"English, please," Adam said.

A look of stubbornness flitted over the woman's delicate face. "Dinner is ready, Silversinger," she repeated in English with a toss of her head. She disappeared into the kitchen in a swirl of wide calico skirts.

Adam looked puzzled by her behavior, but Cat's initial impression was confirmed. Maria Tso was jealous of her for some reason, and Adam was completely unaware of it.

Dinner was a quiet affair, with only Ben and Maria joining them, since the apprentices were not back yet. Ben and Adam kept up a three-way conversation with Cat, but Maria kept her eyes downcast most of the time and ate in silence. The few times she did look up, her eyes darted toward Adam. Cat realized that the woman's snubbing was not as willful as it appeared, for Adam's nearness blinded Maria to the presence of everyone else.

I wonder if Adam knows, Cat asked herself. She thought he'd have to be as blind as Ben, not to notice, yet he wouldn't be the first man to remain happily oblivious to the heart some unfortunate woman wore on her sleeve.

"It's been a long day," Adam said as they finished their after-dinner coffee. Ben had excused himself to finish the necklace he was crafting and Maria was clattering dishes in the kitchen. "As soon as Ben is done with his piece, we'll go back to our hogan for the night. Why don't you go on to bed? You look ready to drop."

Before Cat could answer, the old man returned to the room. He came through the doorway with the same inherent grace she had noted in both Adam and Maria. She never would have guessed from his confident stride that he couldn't see.

"Here, Catriona Frazer. I started making this for you when Adam sent word you would be coming to Peshlakai." He held out a delicate necklace of curved silver bands set with a large sky-blue turquoise in the center. In the middle of the gem, a small curving V of black matrix gave the effect of a gull silhouetted against a clear summer sky. Every line was clean and elegant, and the very simplicity of the design showed that Ben was a master craftsman.

"Oh, Ben," Cat said softly as he put the piece of jewelry into her outstretched hands.

"In my younger days," Ben said, "I wanted to

bend the silver and cut the stones to fit my design, so I worked most of my life inlaying small stones in the Zuni fashion. Now, I can no longer work with the tiny stones, and I have returned to the Navaho style. Now the stone tells me how *it* wishes to be set." He laughed. "Nature always wins, and perhaps it is better so."

Cat tried to thank him, but Adam put a hand on her arm and shook his head. Ben saw the shadowy movements and interpreted them correctly.

"It is all right, Silversinger. I have long since grown used to the ways of the Bellicani." Ben turned his head to Cat. "No thanks are necessary. It is not our way." With a nod he said good night and left the room. Maria came out of the kitchen then and said she was going back to the woman's hogan.

"More coffee?" Adam asked as he picked up the pot.

"No, thanks. Or shouldn't I say that either?" Cat asked in bewilderment.

"You can say anything you want, to me," he teased. "But among The People, we do not thank each other for a small favor. We save our words of gratitude for special occasions."

Cat shrugged her shoulders. "I'll learn," she said, and then danced over to the small mirror hanging on the wall where she fastened the necklace around her throat. The silver arcs made her skin seem whiter and the turquoise made her eyes sparkle with blue-green lights. She whirled around to face Adam. "Isn't it marvelous! Look how the silver flows." She touched the gleaming metal at her throat. "It makes me feel pagan, like some ancient Celtic princess."

She laughed at her imagery and tried to remove the necklace, but the hooked end of the hand-wrought clasp caught in her hair. The more she sought to free it, the worse it became ensnared.

"Need help?" Adam came up behind her, all six-foot-plus of lean height looming over her as he bent and tried to free the necklace from her long curls. Cat could smell the masculine amberwood of his after-shave as he leaned nearer and his breath tickled her ear, sending a shiver of pleasure along her spine.

Then the clasp was freed from her hair and the necklace slid forward. Instantly one of Adam's strong hands swept around to catch it, and the warm touch of it against her bare skin flooded Cat with waves of conflicting feelings that battered her senses. While her mind warned her that it was too soon, her body betrayed her. With a sigh she leaned back against Adam, and his tall form molded intimately against hers so that the barrier of cloth that separated them was as nothing. She felt his powerful thigh muscles and heard the hammering of his heart vibrating through her skin, while his hands swept along her arms in slow gliding movements. Gliding, promising. Slowly he grasped her shoulders and turned her around to face him. His fingers dug into her flesh and the look on his face was one of such urgent hunger that it both frightened and exhilarated her.

Without warning, Adam thrust Cat away from

him with an oath, and was gone. Her skin still tingled from his touch when the sound of the slamming door reached her ears.

Lying awake on the cool sheets of her bed, Cat stared at the shadows on the beamed ceiling, her mind filled with thoughts of Adam and the memory of his touch. The whole room seemed haunted by his presence, the very air to carry his now-familiar scent, and she wondered if he had given his room up to her. And why.

A cool breeze blew softly through the screened windows, ruffling her hair as she tossed and turned. She turned over again. Damn. She pushed back the sheet and sat up on the edge of the bed. What is the matter with you, Catriona Frazer? she scolded herself. But she knew. Adam Hawk was the matter. Walking across the room, she peered through the window at the starry sky, trying to put Adam out of her mind, but she kept remembering the way his strong arms had held her, the way his warm lips had come down on her own. She sighed and opened the door that led to the side veranda.

The night beckoned her, calling out to the restless spirit that moved her, and Cat heeded that primitive summons. She slipped into a pair of sandals and pulled on a light, insubstantial robe. The whole world seemed to hold its breath as she walked through the silent star shine. After she'd gone a few yards, Cat began to feel exposed, out alone with the flatland stretching endlessly on before her. Seeing shelter in a gnarled tree that grew beside a tumble of limestone above the dry wash, she moved quickly toward it.

She heard a sound. Something moving in the brush nearby, and her heart sped up alarmingly. Wolves! she thought. Were there wolves in Arizona? She didn't remember, and now was not the time to find out. She was almost to the shadow of the tree, but decided to turn back. As Cat moved, her foot kicked loose a stone and it fell down the side of the wash, bringing sand and other pebbles down in its wake. She gasped as a hand shot out of the shadows, imprisoning her wrist in a hard grasp.

"What are you doing out here alone at this time of night?" Adam's tone was angry and she felt a twinge of fear as he stepped away from the tree where he had been concealed. He looked as dark and shadowy and mysterious as the night.

"*Oh!*" Cat's heart slammed against her ribs and for a moment she was shocked speechless. "What are *you* doing out here? You scared me out of my wits."

He moved and the starlight fell more strongly on his high-planed cheeks, hiding his eyes, as his other hand came up to rest on her shoulder. "Didn't you see me?" His voice was mocking, filled with disbelief. "Or did you just happen to take a little midnight stroll dressed in that skimpy bit of gossamer?"

The moon escaped from its net of clouds, outlining the sternness of Adam's jaw with silver and polishing his hair to jet. There was nothing soft or tender in the face Cat saw looking down at her.

"You might as well be naked." He bit the words out harshly, and she glanced down.

He was right. Between the moonlight and the playful breeze that pressed the sheer fabric to every curve of her body, there was definitely more of Cat Frazer revealed than she'd realized. "Let me go," she demanded, trying to pull free. But Adam only tightened his grip.

"Is that really what you want?" They stood inches apart in the bright moonlight, Adam's blue eyes challenging her with an expression Cat couldn't—or wouldn't—understand.

"What do you mean?"

"You know damned well what I mean," he countered. "Were you really just taking a walk? Or did you come outside knowing I was here, and just loose your nerve at the last minute?" He put both hands on her shoulders and pulled her against his chest. "Isn't it a little late to get cold feet, Cat?" he added softly in a tone that left no doubt as to his meaning.

He held her fast in his strong arms, crushing her against him, and his mouth came down bruisingly on hers. Cat was too angry to respond to his kiss in the way she usually did. She struggled against him, but he didn't release her until she stepped down on his instep as hard as she could. Her sandals were no match for his leather boots, but he got the message. His hands fell to his sides, and as she whirled around, Cat saw the look of disdain on his face.

She ran as fast as she could over the uneven terrain, her sandals slipping in the loose sand that covered the flinty soil. A few feet ahead of her an owl glided down on silent wings and scooped a field mouse up in its glinting three-inch talons. Cat gasped in dismay, and a protruding root caught her foot. She went down, twisting her ankle as she fell.

Shaking herself, she rose awkwardly and attempted to limp on, but Adam was there in a split second, scooping her up with the same ease the owl had shown in capturing its hapless victim. For a moment he held her so tightly she couldn't speak, couldn't breathe. She listened to the rapid hammering of her own heart in counterpoint to the strong, steady beat of his.

"Put me down," she demanded when she got her wind back again. There was no answer as Adam carried her over the ground smoothly in long, gliding strides that brought them quickly to the veranda. Without a pause, he carried her right up to the door to her room, turned the handle, and went inside. He placed her carefully on the bed, then reached over and turned on the lamp.

"Where does it hurt?" he asked as he prodded her ankle cautiously, watching her face for signs of pain or discomfort.

"It *doesn't* hurt. I tried to tell you that, but you knocked the breath out of me and I could hardly talk."

Adam's face, so cool and impersonal a moment before, was transformed by the wry smile that lifted the corners of his firmly chiseled mouth. "And," he said to her with a sardonic lift of one dark brow, "you don't think you took *my* breath away? Coming to me in the moonlight dressed, or rather *un*dressed, as you are!" His glance flickered over her from head to toe. "God knows I'm not a saint, Catriona Frazer." Although he still smiled, his face darkened with the rush of hot blood that suffused his cheeks.

Cat reached for the top sheet, but Adam grabbed the hem first and floated the snowy linen over her, covering her to the shoulders. "That's better," he said. "I'll make a pact with you. I promise not to sweep you off your feet again, and you promise to stop tormenting me by parading around in that wisp of nothing you call a nightgown."

"I was not parading," Cat replied in a positive fury. "I didn't think anyone else would be awake."

"*Strolling*, then." His eyes crinkled at the corners. "Is it a deal?" He held out a hand to her.

Dammit, he's laughing at me again! Cat gritted her teeth and tried to resist Adam's smile, but something about that crooked grin melted her heart. She held out her hand to him and it disappeared in his large one.

"Friends?"

"Friends." She hoped she wouldn't regret it. Cat had expected a handshake, but instead he simply held her hand in his warm grasp.

"I knew from your silverwork just how your hands would look: small and sensitive, yet capable; strong, yet delicate." He saw the surprised look on her face. "It shows in every line of your jewelry," he told her. "I remember the first time I saw something you'd crafted," he added. "It was a necklace at the Oldford Gallery. A few weeks later I saw the

Narcissus mirror at Ormsby's in Toronto. That's when it first began."

Cat's curiosity, like that of her proverbial namesake, was piqued. "When what began?"

"I think," Adam said as he lifted Cat's hand, "that's when I first began to fall in love with you." He dropped a light kiss into her upturned palm. Then he was on his feet and out of the room before she had time to react, leaving Cat alone with her thoughts and the warm imprint of his lips burning her hand like an invisible brand.

Chapter Six

Breakfast would have been something of a trial except for the calm presence of Ben Slowhorse and the nonstop talkativeness of Cat's apprentice. Joseph Osborne, black eyes in a round face bright with intelligence, badgered Cat for information about everything he could think of, from questions about the Great Lakes region to her opinion of how the Detroit Tigers would fare in the pennant race.

"Give her a chance to eat," Adam protested as he passed the plate of corncakes to Cat.

"Oh, I'm sorry," Joseph said contritely. "It's just that I don't have a chance to talk with someone from off the reservation often. I've only been to Flagstaff and Gallup. And Sedona for the big Art and Craft Exhibit the Gerisches have at their shop in September. Have you ever been to Sedona? What are you going to enter in the show?"

"How are we going to fatten Cat up if you won't let her take a bite without interrupting with questions?"

"I don't want to fatten up," Cat exclaimed while Joseph flushed in embarrassment. "It took me two months to get my weight down right where I want it."

"Too thin for my taste," Adam teased, but with a note of truth in his voice. "You'd look healthier if you put on about ten pounds."

Cat bit her tongue as she poured herself another cup of coffee, dribbling a few drops on the sides of the cup as she fought to control her rising temper. Why is it he can make me so angry, so quickly? And over nothing, really. "I like myself just the way I am, thank you." She smiled sweetly, but Adam was not fooled for a minute and his own smile widened.

"That's why I like you," he told her. "No false modesty."

Cat looked up in time to intercept the glance Maria sent her way, and was surprised by what she saw. There was neither jealousy nor hostility in the dark eyes regarding her, but rather a look of gentle anxiety that Cat was unable to interpret before Maria hastily looked down and passed the plate of corncakes to Ben.

Thank God for corncakes, Cat said to herself. Whatever would we do without them to get over awkward moments!

At that moment, Lee Chen slid into her seat without greeting anyone and filled her mug with coffee. She was a small-boned young woman of about twenty-four years and would have been lovely, with her melting black eyes and fine features, if not for the air of sullen hostility that she wrapped around herself like a cocoon. Lee Chen barely acknowledged the introduction to Cat and dismissed a comment of Joseph's scathingly.

"Put some sugar in your coffee," Joseph

snapped back. "You're as sour as a lemon this morning." Lee's air of cool composure evaporated as she berated the grinning Joseph. The scene threatened to deteriorate into a childish battle between the two young people until Adam quelled any further skirmishes with a sharp word. He rose to his feet.

"Time to break in the new instructor," he said with a note of finality. As they went toward the workroom, Cat could hear Maria and Lee talking over their coffee in the activities room. She had no doubt they were discussing her, and she wondered what they were saying. From the angry sound of Lee's voice, it couldn't be good.

Joseph showed her a belt buckle he had made. A silver rectangle, it was set with pieces of coral, polished white shell, and turquoise. Each piece was surrounded by thin strips of silver in the method known as Zuni channel-inlay. It was cool and smooth as glass, the metal and stones ground and polished to form one silken surface. Cat was impressed.

"This is lovely, Joseph. The technical work is very well done, and I like the zig-zag design of the stones. If this is an example of your jewelry, it will be a real pleasure to work with you."

The apprentice blushed and Cat warmed even more to this impetuous and rather shy apprentice. Although he looked about Lee Chen's age, his boyish eagerness for approval made him seem younger.

But it didn't take Cat long to realize there was some friction between Adam and her young apprentice. Joseph seemed more cheerful after their talk and they went over to watch Ben at work for a while.

"In the old days," Ben told Cat, "the silver was heated over charcoal fires and I used an old tree stump to hammer the metals. Now"—he waved a graceful hand over his modern workbench—"I plug the electric crucible and the soldering iron into the outlet, and the generator gives me all the controlled heat I need to work the silver." He grinned at Cat. "White man's magic," he said. "Good magic."

Ben showed her one of his pieces, which looked like a wide and oddly shaped man's cuff bracelet with a massive blue-green turquoise in the center. "That piece is a *ketoh*, a bow-guard," Joseph said, coming to stand next to her. "It protects the wearer's arm from the recoil of a bowstring. A few years ago the only ones I saw were antiques. But we're getting more orders for them as people turn back to the old practices of the Navaho Way."

"It's exquisite," Cat exclaimed.

Joseph touched a finger to the *ketoh* and traced the elegant lines almost reluctantly. Adam's voice came from over Cat's shoulder. "That's what you should be striving for, Joseph," he said sternly. "Not that shoddy trash you turned out a few weeks ago."

Joseph moved quietly over to his work area, and Cat followed. He turned to her and explained, "I met this girl in Chinle. Her name is Ramona Bluewing, and we want to get married. She has lived in Chicago since she was two, but when the aunt she lived with died last month, she had to come back to the reservation." Joseph picked up a thin gauged piece of silver wire and absently twisted it around his finger. "Ramona . . . Ramona doesn't want to live on the reservation. She isn't used to this kind of life."

Cat felt a pang of pity for Joseph, torn between his love for Ramona and pride in his heritage. She could also identify with the shock of a young woman raised in the Midwest and then suddenly thrust into the unfamiliar life of the reservation. And she would have liked to kick Adam. Joseph was confused, and Adam was handling him in the worst way possible! Surely he should understand how difficult it was to try and support oneself making jewelry.

But Joseph wasn't finished. "Ramona knows a trader in Flagstaff who will furnish the silver and other supplies for me if I make the kind of stuff he wants," he added. "He doesn't pay a lot for individual items, but I can knock out enough pieces to make it worth it. Adam says if I do that, I'm through at Peshlakai. He almost dismissed me on the spot, and I think he's still considering kicking me out of the apprentice program."

"Well," Cat reminded him, "Adam is in charge of the school, but as my own apprentice, you are bound to me, and Adam can't dismiss you without my consent." She'd have to talk to Adam about this matter.

Clearly, while she was here to teach, she was also here to learn. And her first lesson was that it was going to be hard to keep her mouth shut when she felt Adam was hasty or unjust in dealing with Joseph. Cat had no doubt there would be sparks flying when she and Adam clashed, and she almost relished the thought!

That afternoon on her way to dinner Cat poked her head into the weaving room, but it was empty. The rug she'd admired the day before was spotlighted by a brilliant sunbeam and the colors glowed in response. On impulse, she reached up and ran her hand over the surface of the rug, and then heard soft footsteps behind her.

"You think that is a beautiful rug, don't you?" Lee Chen said as Cat turned.

"Yes, I do. Did you make it, Lee?"

The other woman watched Cat for a few seconds, her face a carefully controlled mask that completely hid her thoughts. "No," she finally said with a note of malicious triumph in her voice. "Adam Silversinger's wife made it." She turned and was gone as quietly as she had come.

Round and round the words danced in Cat's head: "Adam's wife." Who was she? Why wasn't she here at Peshlakai with him?

Cat leaned against the wall for support. How could he have kissed her that way when he had a wife? Anger and disillusionment threatened to overwhelm her, but she fought for control. It wasn't possible, she told herself. She knew Adam well enough to realize he was not the kind of man who played around. There must be another explanation.

She wanted some answers desperately. She

wanted to know, but she had to pick the time and place carefully. The important thing was to cool down first.

Returning to the studio, she glanced at Adam from under her lashes, as she worked. He was so handsome he took her breath away, despite her carefully concealed wrath. Even now, while he was laughing at something Ben said, she perceived a sense of sadness just below the surface, a certain vulnerability that showed in the angle of his jaw and the shadowed look in his eyes. Despite her tangled emotions, Cat wished she could do something to ease that look. She realized she was staring at him, and just then he looked over at her.

"Tired, Cat? You look like you're in a trance."

"Just woolgathering, I guess," she answered as he came over to her.

"Take a walk with me, Cat."

She couldn't think of a legitimate reason to refuse, but when he took her hand to help her rise, she snatched it away from him. He looked surprised. Cat stepped out on to the veranda, and Adam followed her in silence.

"Let's just walk for a while," she finally said. He nodded, and they headed out away from the settlement. Cat's emotions were in a turmoil; she knew she had to confront Adam, but somehow, being so close to him made that task too difficult. He completely unnerved her and they had walked for quite a while before Cat looked around and noticed how far they had come. She stopped and Adam turned to take her hands.

"What is it, Cat?" he asked. "Is it about last night? I've wanted to apologize, but we just didn't have a chance to be alone all day."

"I'm just tired," she answered, taking back her hands as she turned away from him. He was giving her the perfect opportunity to ask about his wife and she was freezing up, just letting it slip by. She realized she was frightened of his answer, but she *had* to know. She shook herself slightly and turned to face Adam again. "I'm sorry, Adam, I'm not just tired. There *is* something bothering me." His forehead creased as he looked at her questioningly. "It's something I have to know." She paused to take a deep breath and looked deeply into his eyes. "Adam, where is your wife?"

Adam's face changed, becoming as hard and unyielding as the land that surrounded them. He turned away from her almost violently, but she could see the pulse beating at his temple. She waited silently.

Adam didn't answer, and the eyes that had been so clear and blue were now cold and hard as flint. He avoided looking at her.

Finally, she could stand the silence no longer. "Adam. I'm sorry—" She put out her hand blindly.

"No," he said quietly. "I'm the one who's sorry." The hard lines of his face eased. "I shouldn't have reacted as I did. My wife," he answered softly. "My wife is dead."

Cat wished she'd never opened her mouth. She wished she could erase the look of pain that crossed Adam's face as he spoke. She ached to reach out and touch him, to hold out her arms and comfort him. But she had ventured, unasked, into his personal hell, and would intrude no further without his permission.

"I'm truly sorry, Adam. I didn't mean to pry."

"No, Catriona Frazer. You raised the question of my wife, and now you shall listen to my answer. Then perhaps I can put the past behind me and go on to the future." He took her hand and pulled her down beside him, and as he poured out his story, Cat wondered if he had ever really talked out his pain and sorrow with anyone before.

"We met at a dance over at Window Rock. I thought she was the most beautiful girl I'd ever seen, as graceful as a butterfly. Her name was Theresa, and before the night was over, I asked her if she would take me for her husband. When she looked down at her feet so shyly and whispered, 'Yes,' I could hardly believe my ears.

"Her father liked me, but her mother wasn't pleased to have a son-in-law who walked so much in the Anglo world. I told her I would build a hogan next to hers and live in the old ways that meant so much to that family."

Cat had seen clusters of hogans from time to time as they neared Peshlakai yesterday, and remembered that life centered around the wife's family. On the reservation, daughters usually stayed on as part of an extended family with their husbands and children, while sons went off after marriage to live with their wives' relatives. It was hard for Cat to picture Adam in that type of setting.

"Soon after we were married," he continued, digging at the earth with a small stick of juniper, "it was discovered that Theresa had a problem with her heart. Defective valves from rheumatic fever. That's what eventually killed her."

"Wasn't there anything the doctors could do? I thought—"

"Doctors?" Adam interrupted her, lines of bitterness carved at the corners of his mouth. "She followed the old ways like her mother, but they held no cure for her illness. Theresa refused to have any tests or go to a clinic. She was horrified when I suggested she consider having surgery. Wayne Yazzie came back here to practice medicine and he told us surgery was her only hope. Theresa said she would rather die. So she did." The stick tore into the soil and splintered into sharp fragments. Cat listened in anguished silence to the rest of his story.

"I was making a necklace for her. It was to be a surprise, and I worked on it while she baked bread in the stone oven outside. Fifteen minutes later I went out and I found her . . ."

Cat didn't know what to do, what to say. "You still love her very much." The words came unbidden from some deep place where sympathy mingled with an odd ache.

"Love her! I did once. But when she died, I *hated* her." He looked full at Cat then. "I hated her because she died and left me. I hated her because her stubborn fears killed her. And I hated her because I thought those fears were greater than her love for me."

"But you don't hate her now." Again her heart spoke for her.

Adam sighed. "No. I don't hate her now. I'm used to being alone. But when she died, I left the reservation. I went out into the Anglo world and tried to turn my back on all the old ways. In the end I had to come back. It is where I belong." He stood up. "I'm sorry. You asked me a simple question and I gave you a soap opera." Then he smiled, a proud but almost shy smile. "I've never been able to say all of that to anyone before. Thank you, Cat."

She rose and took his hand and he placed his other one over hers. They stood a moment, looking into each other's eyes, completely at peace with each other. Cat was filled with a joy and contentment so fierce it frightened her. She kept silent, knowing she would burst into tears if she tried to speak. She didn't completely understand the emotions that surged through her, but she didn't need to understand. It was enough to feel.

When they returned to the main house, the subtle change in their relationship was apparent to the others. Maria looked sad but resigned, Lee angry, and Ben and Joseph amused. They had been gone quite a while and it finally dawned on Cat that the others thought she and Adam had become lovers. Although nothing like that had transpired between them, Cat realized that she and Adam had crossed over some invisible line. It was only a matter of time, she knew, a very short time, before they would truly become lovers in every meaning of the word.

Chapter Seven

From the moment Adam suggested they visit the White Ruins Canyon, Cat knew that the moment had come. And by her acceptance of his invitation, she consciously acknowledged her readiness for the next step in their relationship.

She had never been more nervous in her life. She showered and powdered herself, feeling like a girl on her first date, or a bride on her wedding night, and the thought made her giggle. Then she thought, Maybe I'm wrong, maybe this is nothing more than a picnic. But her feminine instincts decried that idea. Since her talk with Adam, their relationship had changed entirely. They were so in tune that in the workshop they'd often said the same thing at the same time, much to the delight of Joseph, who followed this romance closely. But, most often, when Cat and Adam worked together, words were unnecessary. Her eyes sought him a thousand times a day, and she usually found him watching her. She delighted in his every movement, every aspect of his face. As if by some silent agreement, they had avoided touching each other in even the most casual way. It heightened the tension and promised a feast after the short fast.

A rap on the door signaled Adam's arrival, and Cat started, tangling the hairbrush in her long copper hair.

"You're just in time to rescue me," she announced, and turned around so he could unsnarl the brush from her curls. His hands, in her hair, sent delicious chills down her back and arms. Every inch of her skin was alive and reveling in the magnetic aura of his nearness. His touch was gentle, but she knew that he, too, was caught up in the magic of their togetherness.

Freeing the lock of hair, Adam lifted it and kissed it. "You have such beautiful hair! That first time I saw you, at the gallery, I wanted to pull the pins out and see it tumbling loosely over your shoulders like this." He tangled both his hands in it, bringing her face up as he leaned closer. "Cat . . ." he began doubtfully, but she didn't let him finish his question.

Instead, she leaned her head against his chest and slid her arms around his lean waist. His arms came around and held her tightly while his cheek lowered to rest on the top of her hair. They stood like that awhile, completely content to do nothing more for the moment, and then Cat reluctantly pulled away, smiling up at him.

"You said there was a pool there. Can we swim in it?"

Her tone, words, and eyes were all invitation.

"Do you have a suit?" he asked with a quirk of one dark eyebrow.

"Of course not." She laughed softly, widening her smile.

"Then we'd better get out of here," he said with a laugh. "Or we'll never get out of here!"

An hour and a half later they were driving across the flat plain toward the distant spires. Adam pointed to the left. "White Ruins Canyon."

Cat strained her eyes, but the land ahead seemed flat and featureless. She was wondering where the ruins were when the earth suddenly seemed to open up before them. A deep chasm cut into the earth, and a great natural cave ran along the west wall, its span filled with crumbling ruins of mud brick.

Adam led the way down, and although the going was tricky in a few places, he knew the quickest and safest route. They came to a ledge and she could see the ruins clearly, but he led her around a curve in the opposite direction. There, they came to a place where a rock slide had dislodged the footpath.

"Jump and I'll catch you," Adam told her. She would have jumped a hundred feet if he'd asked her to, so great was her trust in him.

When he caught her about the waist, the touch of his hands seemed to burn through her clothes to her skin, and she caught her breath raggedly. Instantly she was pulled tight against him and his mouth came down on hers with a ruthless hunger that matched her own. She opened her lips to his probing tongue, too greedy to want or need a more gentle kiss. As the kiss deepened, Adam's hands moved up and down her back in slow movements, and Cat pressed her body against his. Adam groaned from deep within. Cat could feel the sound reverberate through his chest, and her nipples tingled and swelled in response. Adam lifted his head an instant, then planted one more quick kiss on her soft lips. When he spoke, his voice was shaky with longing.

"Do you want to go on?" He looked at her searchingly, as if all the world depended on her answer. Did he mean go on with the kiss, or with their visit to the ruins? It didn't matter: where he led, she would follow, unassailed by doubt or reservation. She loved him. It was as simple as that.

She nodded, and Adam took her hand, lifting up the palm to receive the warm imprint of his lips. Without a word and still holding her hand, he drew her along the path behind him.

They walked for a while longer, moving quickly and gracefully, like two dancers who had moved together a thousand times. He had moved so that he was two steps ahead of her. He was staying close to the rock. And then suddenly he was gone.

"Adam?" No answer. She'd be damned if she'd go hunting for him while he played silly games. Then she heard his voice as if from a great distance, and she spotted a crevasse covered with mesquite and juniper. Cat worked her way through the opening, which led to a natural ramp leading gently downward. At the end of the rocky tunnel, she came to an arch that opened on another world.

Her first reaction was amazement. They were on the floor of a small valley hidden by the overhanging rock and protected from above by the inward curve of the sheer walls. Vegetation screened the top, but pale sunlight filtered through. A wide pool, blue as a morning glory, lay in the center, the water pure and crystalline. Adam stood a few yards away, and Cat realized he had not been hiding. He was only lost in thought. Or perhaps memory.

Hearing her behind him, he turned and smiled. "Do you like my surprise? Very few people know about it, even among The People. And no anthropologists or archaeologists even dream it exists." He took off the leather knapsack that held their sandwiches and motioned for Cat to be seated on the mossy ground. She didn't move and he looked at her questioningly, a pleased smile still hovering on his lips. His eyes looked like sapphires against his gold-brown skin.

Cat stepped closer and was instantly swept into his arms. It seemed the most natural thing in the world when she began undoing his buttons, one by one. He laughed in surprise and delight, and then it became a race to see who could unbutton the other one's shirt first. Neither one of them paid any attention to who actually won, for the sensation of burning flesh against flesh left them both breathless. His hands roved over the satiny skin of her bare back tenderly while they exchanged deep exploring kisses.

Adam leaned her back against the hardness of his arm while his other hand moved around to clasp her soft breast, rubbing his palm lightly over the straining tip as he caressed it. Cat melted into his embrace, sliding both arms around his neck and arching her back instinctively to thrust her breasts against him more. She heard him gasp, and the hand that had fondled so gently became more urgent.

"Adam, Adam . . ." she murmured against him, her mouth moving softly over his skin, leaving a trail of kisses across his chest as the world blurred and shifted around them. Somehow, without once loosening his iron embrace, she found that Adam had lowered her to the mossy ground beside the blue water. His mouth lightly touched the line of her jaw, nipping and seeking, as his lips moved down the curve of her throat and into the valley between her breasts.

The tingling of his breath against her naked skin sent ripples of excitement cresting through her body, and she felt herself lifted, carried away on a tidal wave of love and desire. She pulled his head against her, and the warmth of his lips, the cool flick of his tongue across her tender flesh sent a shock of ecstasy radiating out and then down her spine. His mouth claimed her sensitive nipple, teasing it lightly. His kisses trailed across to her other breast, where he roused the ripe tip with his teeth and tongue until Cat's pulses pounded and her blood sang in her ears like wild music. Her hands wandered the expanse of his chest, feeling the rippling muscle beneath, then raking down his sides and around to his back. She wanted him closer, wanted to feel the heat of his body melting into hers.

Adam's mouth hunted lower, softly grazing the skin down to her waist until his hands deftly unclasped her belt buckle. Impatient of the barrier of cloth between them, Cat pushed at the waistband of her Levi's, but Adam's hands were there first. As he slid her jeans down, his kisses followed, and the touch of his lips along the softness of her abdomen made Cat shiver with anticipation.

In a moment, his clothes were discarded too. His knee slid between hers, but she needed no urging. She welcomed its weight upon her as she returned his kisses with an intensity and passion she had never known could exist. His hands moved knowingly over her, rousing sensations that almost overwhelmed Cat. She clutched at his shoulders, but he only kissed her, delaying the final act. His lips traveled over her temple, then touched her eyelids gently. She opened her eyes to see his face filled with tenderness, flushed with desire, and she knew in a woman's way that he wanted to know, *needed* to know, that she was sure of what she was doing.

She smiled at him, a ripe and knowing smile as old as Eve. He read the message there. Once more his lips roved lower, kissing the gentle slope of her abdomen while she tangled her fingers in his dark hair. Once again he brought her to the brink of rapture, and Cat felt she could no longer endure such joyous torture. He proved her wrong, and his caressing hands and mouth brought to her the very height of passion, so that her desperate need for him was almost a pain. She cried out his name and welcomed him as the world erupted in waves of delight. She and Adam were one, their every movement synchronized as they gave full rein to passion. They were in a world where no one else could follow, lost and exaulted in the joy of their love.

Afterward, they lay beside the pool, wrapped in each other's arms, and in each other's dreams. They smiled and kissed and talked. After they ate, they made love again, as if it were the first time since the world had begun. For them, it was.

Chapter Eight

When they returned to Peshlakai, Cat was sure her face would give them away. No one said anything to them, then or later, but from that night on, Adam and Cat shared the big bedroom that had once been his alone.

Cat was rapidly adjusting to life on the reservation. Although her eyes still longed for the sight of water and green trees, her happiness with Adam more than made up for that lack. "I can't believe how happy I am," she said to him one morning. "I feel a little guilty about it. At the very least, I should feel like a scarlet woman." She laughed.

"No," Adam corrected as he dropped a kiss on her soft lips. "You should feel like a very *loved* woman. Silversinger's woman." He kissed her again, and they were almost late for breakfast after one thing led to the inevitable other.

Life was running smoothly for Cat as she basked in Adam's love. She was prepared to love him and all the world in return. Strangely, Maria's jealousy seemed to evaporate, and finally Cat realized it had only been the love of a friend who worried that Adam would be hurt again, not the romantic love of a woman for a man.

Even Lee Chen seemed to accept her. Cat was shrewd enough to see that the escalating battles between Lee and Joseph had taken on all the aspects of a courtship ritual, at least where Lee was concerned. Whether Joseph was still in thrall to the resourceful Ramona was something only time would reveal.

The only problems they encountered came about when Cat's quick temper ran afoul of Adam's often autocratic manner. When these attributes clashed, sparks flew and the others slipped silently away. Unlike their initial argument over her apprentice, Adam usually won. Cat was still cautious of the new bond between them, and too much in love with him to press the issues. Unfortunately, this left a residual of growing frustration that Cat, unwisely, choose to ignore. The little things began to add up here and there, and the unacknowledged tension built up beneath the surface.

As the days passed, Cat learned the genesis of Adam's name. Like many Navaho smiths, he liked to sing as he worked, and his vibrant voice often filled the workroom. She thought he might have become a professional singer as his mother had, if he'd been so inclined.

One golden morning eight weeks later, they were alone in the workroom, and Adam sang for Cat, making up melodies and inventing silly lyrics to make her laugh.

At that time, Cat was making great progress on the piece she was planning to enter in the prestigious September Art and Craft Show in Sedona. It was really more of a wide flat collar, than a necklace. Composed of a network of gold and silver wire, it was as delicate and airy as antique lace. For accent she had included small polished stones of obsidian, the volcanic glass that appeared black until held to the light. Then its true color could be seen, glowing like dark honey.

Apache Tears. That's what the stones were called, and Cat had fallen in love with the legend, that they were formed from tears of grief when the Apache Nation was forced from its land by advancing waves of settlers.

She intended the necklace to symbolize the beauty and simplicity of Indian life lived in partnership with nature, but it was more than that; it was a reflection of her love for Adam, and the spirit of that love was shown in every line of the necklace.

Now, as she soldered the intricate framework of silver and gold wire pieces, Adam came up behind her.

His movements were as soft and silent as ever, but they never startled her anymore. She was in tune with him and always sensed his presence as the communion of spirit between them deepened with each passing day.

"I think, when you are finished, that necklace will be the best thing you have ever done." He placed his hands gently on either side of her waist and whispered in her ear, but the words were obscured by the sound of the screen door banging loudly.

Lee Chen came into the room, a scowl marring

her lovely face as she approached them. Without a word, she upended a paper bag and spilled several objects out on top of Cat's worktable.

Wordlessly Adam picked up a silver case for a cigarette lighter, garishly studded with bits of cheap turquoise, heavily impregnated with wax. He looked inside for a name or symbol indicating the smith. But as Cat saw herself when she picked up the piece, there was no mark.

"Where did you get this?" Adam asked, his face still and his eyes masked. He flicked a finger at the red and white bag that had OTTO'S GENUINE INDIAN CRAFTS written boldly across the front.

"I found them in Gallup this morning," Lee said, her lips compressed into a tight line.

There was an undercurrent Cat was unable to read passing between the other two. "I don't understand," she mumbled, half to herself. She picked up a ring, poorly designed and executed with coral and shell in the likeness of a Hopi Kachina mask.

Adam slammed his hand down on the tabletop, and the absence of any emotion in his face made the violent movement all the more emphatic. "I understand," he said in a voice low with repressed anger. "I understand only too well! Where is he?"

"Gone to Kayenta with Ben," Lee answered. Suddenly, Cat felt like an outsider again. They spoke in English, but they might as well have been speaking in the Navaho tongue.

"Who are you talking about?" She placed her hand lightly on the arm of Adam's blue cotton workshirt, but he didn't seem aware of her touch.

He threw the cigarette lighter case down. It bounced once, then fell to the floor with a soft tinging sound. Slowly Adam turned to Cat.

"It is a good thing that your other apprentice arrives soon." He spoke each word distinctly and the cadence of his voice had changed, so that the words had a rhythm of their own in the way that Ben's speech did.

"What do you mean?"

"It is good that you will have others to teach, for Joseph Osborne is through here."

"Are you crazy?" She looked at Adam as if he had indeed lost his mind. "Do you think Joseph made these . . . these trashy goods? He's a better workman than that! Besides, there's no name, no silversmith's stamp inside any of these."

"Use your eyes." Adam's voice was now as harsh as his words. "See how the bezel holding the stones is crimped? Only Joseph does them that way. And the way the raised edging is soldered. Can you look at that and tell me you do not know the maker?"

Cat carefully examined the remaining pieces. Yes, the crimping was done in a way she'd never seen anyone but her enthusiastic young apprentice use, a rounded, reverse zigzag that he'd made up himself.

"But surely that isn't enough to prove that this is Joseph's handiwork. Even the soldering—" She broke off as the apprentice came into the room, his face pale beneath his ink-black hair.

"Don't defend me, Cat." He came toward them as if each step caused him agony, but he held his head high. "I made those . . . things." Lee looked from Joseph to Adam, then her eyes locked with Cat's. The girl read the message there and silently slipped from the room.

"Collect your belongings," Adam said in a voice like the crack of a rifle. "I will take you to Window Rock tonight to your mother's hogan."

"I just want to—" Joseph started, but whatever he had to say Adam angrily cut short.

"There is nothing to say. Get your things." He turned away and the young man went to his work station and began to collect his tools.

"Now just a minute!" Cat exploded. "Joseph is *my* apprentice, bound to *me*. I want to know just what the hell is going on here." She turned on Adam. "You can't dismiss *my* apprentice unless I release him." Stunned silence fell over the room like a pall. Cat, her cheeks as flaming as her hair, confronted Adam, who was as pale as death.

"I have spoken." He stalked out of the room and headed toward the door to the outside, but she caught up with him and pulled at his shirt. "Stop!" she commanded.

He stopped. She came around in front of him. The look on his face drove the high color from hers, leaving her as white as he.

"Don't you walk out when I'm talking to you," she said sharply. Although her voice trembled with anger, she was frightened. His blue eyes sparked with the fire of his rage, and he grabbed both her arms above the elbow until she felt bruised to the bone.

"Don't ever challenge me like that again," he hissed, giving her a shake. "Don't *ever* try to humiliate me with your Anglo woman ways again."

Shock drove all the anger from her. Her wonderful world had crumbled around her with the exchange of a few furious words. She fought for breath over the hammering of her heart as she faced the harsh, cold face of a total stranger. But even in her despair, she fought for what she knew was right.

"You haven't even listened to his explanation. You haven't even given him a chance." Although tears blurred her vision, she willed them not to fall and held her chin up defiantly. "If Joseph goes, I go."

She waited to hear the words that would destroy her happiness. Instead, she found herself swept into his arms and held so tightly she couldn't draw a breath. Adam's lips were in her hair, on her face, and then on her lips as he murmured broken words of love and pain.

"Cat . . . oh, God! What did we almost do?" He pulled back and brushed her silky hair away from her wet cheeks, "Cat, I love you. I couldn't bear to lose you over such a stupid thing." His mouth was on hers, warm and hard, seeking reassurance in the soft response of her lips. Not a single sound emanated from the workroom where Joseph awaited his fate.

Cat looked up at Adam and saw that the stranger was gone, leaving only the man she loved. But he was hurt and bewildered. "Oh, Adam! Adam, I love you. I never meant . . ." The words trailed off, for although she hadn't meant to humiliate him, she had meant every word she'd said. They stared at each other a moment, and then his lips quirked in a lopsided smile.

It was true: Joseph *was* her apprentice, bound to her by the rules of their craftsman's guild. Any decision, such as dismissing the young man, had to originate with Cat herself. For several painful seconds, their relationship hung in the balance. Then love tipped the scales.

"You are a stubborn female, Small Heather Woman. But you are right." He sighed. "We will talk to Joseph." Cat smiled back and they went toward the workroom, side by side. She wasn't fooled. He had said they would talk to the apprentice, but if Adam didn't like the young man's answers, there would still be hell to pay.

"We have talked," Adam told Joseph. "Now it is your turn."

"I made those pieces several months ago," Cat's apprentice explained haltingly. "I was just trying to unload them."

Adam looked hard at him for a few seconds. Cat thought that the young man seemed sincere, but she remembered his plans to marry Ramona Bluewing, and she wondered. She hoped with all her heart that he was telling the truth.

"Very well," Adam said, nodding to Cat for confirmation. "We will accept your word, Joseph. But you are here to learn all we can teach you of our craft and you have no time to waste in making shoddy tourist trinkets."

Cat joined in, so the apprentice would know they were of one mind. "You are an artist, Joseph. And anytime you do less than you are capable, it diminishes you. You have great talent. But if you do poor work, your technique will suffer for it. And your spirit will, too."

Adam lifted a small curved bracelet. "This you will recognize as the work of Johnny Manygoats. It is not an expensive piece, yet it is beautifully and skillfully done. Johnny does not insult the visitors who come to buy Navaho jewelry by offering them bad design and tawdry workmanship. Every piece he makes is as carefully done as all the others, no matter what price it will bring from the traders."

Joseph hung his head. Adam's angry words had only brought answering fear, but his words of truth brought shame to the apprentice.

"Thank you," Joseph said. At first Cat was surprised, but then she realized that this indeed was a special favor, one for which it was appropriate for someone of his culture to give thanks. Joseph went back to his worktable, and Cat and Adam returned to theirs.

That evening, after dinner, Cat and Adam lay together on the big bed still dressed, and talked. They talked of everything but the incident earlier that had threatened all they had built together.

"Would you rub my shoulders a little, Adam?" She rolled over on her stomach and he stretched out beside her, massaging her tired muscles with his sensitive hands. "Umhhhhmmmm," she sighed contentedly.

"You are a cat, you know," he teased. "You positively purr when you're stroked and petted."

"Ouch! You're going to have people think you beat me if you keep bruising my arms." He pulled up the full sleeves of her light cotton blouse to disclose several dark blotches.

"Did I do that this afternoon?" He appeared horrified. Kissing the bruised areas, he next began sliding his lips over the warm skin at the nape of her neck, sending little shivers along her back. "Let me make it up to you . . ." He pulled up the hem of her blouse, so that his hands could caress her bare skin. She again felt the callus ridges as they glided over her skin.

"Adam? Where are your horses?" She rolled up on one elbow, but he only continued his tactile inspection of her body from under the front of her blouse. "Ad*am!*" She laughed.

"The horses are at my mother's hogan near Kayenta, you madwoman. What possible interest do you have in horses at a time like this?"

"Well, you must have ridden a lot in the past." She took one of his hands and trailed an index finger lightly across the palm. He didn't answer, didn't move, and at last she looked up.

"Did I bring back a memory? I'm sorry." She sat up enough to reach a hand up to cradle his cheek. "Whiskers. I thought Indian's didn't have any."

He looked down at her with a half-smile, his blue eyes troubled. "No. No memories. My life began again for me when I met you." He took her hand and kissed it.

"What is it? What's bothering you?" she gazed at him intently, as if she would read his mind, and his eyes lowered.

"Nothing, Cat Woman." He pulled her hard against his chest for a moment before pressing her back against the mattress. "Nothing, Small Heather Woman. *Silversinger's Woman.*" His hands were moving over her breasts, arousing her body while they quieted her mind. Her lips opened to receive his kiss, and her thoughts went spinning out of control. The flame of his passion lit an answering fire deep within her, one that blazed hotly until she was consumed by its bright, leaping glory.

When those flames were reduced to contented embers, she lay in his arms half-asleep, dreaming and planning for the future. And she pretended to herself that no snakes had entered their Garden of Eden.

Chapter Nine

It was too hot to work and too hot to relax. Ben had spent the night with relatives at Kayenta, and Joseph and Lee had gone somewhere with a group of young people earlier. Only Cat and Adam were in the workroom.

"Let's go to White Ruins Canyon and forget about working," Adam coaxed her.

"You know I'd love to go, but first I need to get a little more soldered on this necklace. When we break for lunch, we'll go and skinny-dip in the Morning Glory Pool, all right?"

Cat was working on the Apache Tears necklace for the Sedona Art and Craft Show. It was one of the most important events in the southwest for silversmiths, and she was determined to make a good showing. As her relationship with Adam had bloomed, Cat had worked past the emotional block that had hindered her artistic development. She wanted to bring back a prize from Sedona, not merely for herself, but as thanks to Adam for the help he had given her and the faith he had shown in her talent.

"How can I resist such a tempting offer?" Adam said, sliding his arms around her waist. He spun her around and kissed her thoroughly. "That's just the coming attractions," he teased. They were so engrossed in each other they didn't hear the Jeep pulling up until it stopped outside their window. They went out on the veranda together.

"Silversinger!" A tall shapely woman who looked part Indian climbed out of the battered vehicle. Silver earrings dangled like icicles against her smooth chestnut hair, and her wrists and fingers were decked with bangles of every description. A burly fair-haired man climbed out of the driver's seat.

"Linda! George! It's good to see you. What are you doing out here?"

"We're on our way to a Sing out Black Mesa way. Just stopped in to see if you and your wife are going," the man said.

"Actually," Linda confessed, "we just wanted to meet your wife before everyone else did." She smiled warmly at Cat. "We have so looked forward to meeting you, and now we can boast that we were among the first to welcome Silversinger's bride."

"Cat, this is George and Linda Gerisch from Sedona." He turned toward her. "My wife, Cat."

Cat almost choked and felt her face redden with embarrassment. She looked to Adam for help, but there was none forthcoming from that direction. She smiled self-consciously. She didn't know what to say, so she didn't say anything, and instead led the way into the cool interior of the house. Was this one of Adam's jokes?

Cat poured out four mugs of coffee while Adam

fought to keep a smile off his face. I'll kill him, she thought. How could he do this to me?

"Well," George said, "we sold the Concho belt you made, last Thursday. And this morning Linda sold two of your wife's bracelets to a fellow from Texas. A real big spender. He took both your cards, too."

I will definitely kill him. Cat writhed inwardly. The mock-fearful glances Adam sent her way did nothing to assuage her ire. Linda distracted Cat with a few questions about her work, while George and Adam talked business.

"It is *so* good to see him smile again," Linda said almost to herself. That made Cat feel better, but she was still itching to get Adam alone.

"Who is the Sing for?" Adam was asking.

"Eric Bluewing. He got back from the army a few days ago, and they're holding an Enemy Way for him. We heard about it at Goulding's this morning."

Cat listened with interest. She was familiar with the term; an Enemy Way was a ceremonial to remove evil influences and curses the young man might have picked up while he was exposed to the Anglo world. It was a long ceremony, taking three days, but many people just came on the last day, if she remembered correctly.

"Cat and I will be there," Adam said.

Cat found her reactions mixed. She was fascinated by the idea of seeing an Enemy Way—at least as much as someone not of The People would be allowed to witness. But she was miffed that Adam had said they would go without even consulting her, and she was appalled by this business of being called "Adam's wife" without benefit of license or clergy.

"We'll see you there, then," Linda said with a friendly smile. "My dear, I hope you'll be very happy here with Adam." The unexpected guests departed, leaving Adam to face the music alone.

"Adam! Why did you say I was your wife?" Cat didn't know whether to laugh or cry in exasperation.

Adam's eyes laughed at her, but his voice was serious when he answered. "Cat, you know by now that some things are very different on the reservation."

She nodded. At first, she had held the erroneous notion that the Navaho life was just a simpler, somewhat quainter version of life as she knew it. But over the past three months, as she had gotten to know more of The People, she had come to realize it was very different, even alien in its basic principles and practices.

"Well," he continued, "we have no wedding ceremonies like you do in the Anglo world. When a man and woman live together, sleep together, they are considered man and wife." His dark blue eyes watched hers gravely. "Does that upset you?"

She thought a minute before replying. "Not *upset*, exactly. It's just that it takes some getting used to."

"It is known we live together here. When we go

to the Sing, you will be considered my wife. I think you should realize that."

Cat was unsure of her reception of this news. It wasn't the idea of being a wife to Adam that she found disconcerting. That thought had long been on her mind, although he never spoke of any permanent commitment between them. But wasn't that what she hoped for? Was that why he never said anything about marriage to her, even in their most tender moments? Did he truly already consider her his wife?

It was a little daunting to think he might consider her his wife when he had never asked to marry her and she had certainly never given her consent. She looked at him, her green eyes wide and hesitant. They'd have to talk this over.

"Well? Will you go to the Sing with me tonight?" he asked belatedly. The look on his face was unreadable.

"All right. What should I wear?"

He grinned. "I like you best in nothing at all. But I think the red skirt and white blouse would be more suitable."

"And attract less attention."

"You'll attract enough attention as it is," he told her. "We'd better clean up here and get ready. It's about an hour-and-a-half drive to the Bluewings' hogan."

Cat cleared away her work, except the Apache Tears necklace, and went to take a shower. Things were still a little up in the air between them, but she didn't want to force a confrontation that neither of them was prepared to deal with at the moment. She'd go to the Sing and enjoy it. Tomorrow they could talk things over.

"I'm ready," Cat announced as she entered the workshop, dressed in a white cotton blouse and a full skirt of deep red cloth that Lee, in a surprising gesture of friendship, had woven for her. The skirt had a twelve-inch flounced hem that swirled gracefully around her slim ankles as she pivoted around for his inspection.

"You are beautiful," he said in a matter-of-fact way that made the compliment even greater. "All you need are some hard goods to look perfect." Cat knew he was referring to the necklaces, bracelets, belts, and hatbands with which the other guests would be decked. Portable wealth was an important part of their culture, and it was necessary to make a respectable display of such items at important ceremonies, such as the Sing tonight.

"Yes, I wish I had more. I should have kept out one of those necklaces I took to Sedona to wear tonight."

Adam smiled, his white teeth flashing in the bright daylight streaming into the room. He looked dangerously handsome in a black shirt and jeans with a red band tied around his hair. He wore a necklace of his own design and a splendid antique Concho belt. "Turn around. I have a surprise."

Obediently Cat did as she was bid. She felt, rather than heard, him come up behind her in that silent walk she knew so well. He lifted her heavy hair, swinging it in front of her shoulders.

"What are you doing?" She felt him undoing the silver necklace Ben had given her that first night in Peshlakai.

"I have a present for you. Close your eyes."

She closed them, then heard the soft sound of silver pieces hitting each other. His hands went to her throat, warm and strong, and he fastened something cool around her neck. It was long and dangled down between her breasts, and she could feel several larger shapes touching her collarbone and her upper chest. She tried to guess what it would look like.

He steered her to the wall where a long antique mirror hung. "Open your eyes." The low rumble of his voice near her ear filled her with delightful tingles. She opened her eyes.

A necklace. And such a necklace! It was made of round and oval beads interspersed with nuggets of turquoise and it hung almost to her waist. Done in the Navaho squash-blossom style, in place of pomegranate buds, it had eighteen pieces molded in the shape of the lion's-paw seashell, varying from the size of a dime to pieces as large as quarters. Instead of the usual naja, the crescent-shaped piece that traditionally fell from the center, there was a stylized mountain lion. She saw, too, that for all the massive quantity of silver, the design and execution had a light and airy quality highly reminiscent of her own work.

"See what I have learned from you, my love?"

Adam whispered as she smiled delightedly at her image in the mirror. She was speechless with admiration and pleasure for a moment, touching the silver lightly with her sensitive artist's fingers.

"Adam, it's truly a masterpiece."

He nuzzled her neck. "That blouse doesn't show off the necklace well like that," he said, pulling the gathered neckline down around her creamy shoulders. "And you need earrings."

From his pocket, he pulled jacia earrings, made up of hundreds of pieces of shell and ancient turquoise. The tiny beads were strung on several loops of thread for each ear, and hung almost to her shoulders.

"These might have been made for you," he told her. She immediately noticed how the green of her eyes matched the soft green of the stones, changed from their original blue by skin oils through the years. "These belonged to my great-grandmother. And now they are yours."

Cat was touched by his gift, and more than a little fearful of the implications. "What was her name?" she asked, to keep from asking the real question on her mind.

"Maeve Kennedy!" He laughed at her surprise. "The men in my family have a penchant for falling in love with Celtic women," he explained, kissing Cat's shoulder.

"You made that up!" She laughed, pinning the earrings to her ears.

"No, really." He ran his hands lightly up and

down her arms. "But there is still something wrong with that blouse."

Ever so slowly, he reached in front of her and undid the ties that held her blouse together. She watched their reflections in the mirror as he discarded the unwanted garments. Cat saw herself, bare-breasted, wearing his love-gift like some pagan princess carrying her wealth in silver.

As his eyes swept over her image, Cat felt a strange sense of power. She pulled a lock of hair over her shoulder so that it fell in a gleaming haze across one breast, and Adam shivered, pulling her back against his body. He cupped his hands beneath her breasts, and she laid her head back on his shoulder while his lips traced an arc of sweet fire along the soft curve of her throat.

With a soft moan, he spun her around to face him. She tilted her chin up and smiled, green eyes daring, tempting. She saw the rapid rise and fall of his chest, heard his breathing quicken.

She reached behind her back to unbutton her skirt, then pretended to stop. "What if someone should come in?" She looked at him from under her lashes.

"They're all gone, and you know it, you beautiful witch." He took a step forward, but as her hands went back to the buttons, he stopped her.

"Wait." He reached down under the workbench and pulled out a box, his eyes never leaving her. He lifted the lid and brought out a silver Concho belt, designed to match the lovely necklace and studded with green stones in the same color as those that hung from her ears now. He stepped forward and knelt before her, placing the belt around her waist and clasping it with hands that were not quite steady.

"Now," he said, helping her release the skirt and the frothy petticoat she wore beneath it. The garments slid silkily over the lush curve of her hips until they fell in a foamy heap at her bare feet. The bit of sheer fabric remaining was no barrier to his ardor and in seconds it was gone like a wisp of cloud floating to the floor.

"You look like a moon goddess," Adam said huskily. "All ivory and silver except for your flaming hair." Still kneeling, he put his arms around her, and because he was so tall, his dark head rested between her breasts. He pressed his lips to her skin, then covered her breasts with kisses, and she pulled him close. His hands moved slowly over the swell of her hips and down the smooth contours of her legs in soft, sensuous circles.

A shiver of anticipation ran along her limbs as she guided his seeking mouth, and she cried out at the sensations his hands and tongue aroused in her. She twined her hands in his hair and moved against him. Even the texture of his clothing against her flushed skin filled Cat with abandoned delight.

He lifted his face and she rained kisses on his temples, his eyelids, and his warm, hard mouth until it softened beneath hers. Adam stood then, sweeping her up into his arms. As he carried her to the bedroom, she took the end of the long necklace and pulled it over his head.

"Now you're my prisoner," she teased, laughing softly against his ear.

"Yes," he told her, blue eyes blazing into hers. "From the moment I first saw you, beautiful and angry and spitting fire!" He went in the open doorway and didn't even bother to close it behind him. Still holding her against him, he knelt down and stretched out beside her on the sheepskin rug. Then his long hands were at her waist, tugging at the belt clasp. "You don't need anything to make you beautiful," he said, discarding the belt.

"I need you, Adam" she whispered. "I need you . . ."

His mouth was over hers, drinking its wine as he kissed her deeply.

The thin veneer of civilization slipped away from her as easily as the unwanted clothing dropped from his lean, muscular body. In seconds she felt the hard length of him against her and knew the urgency of his desire. She welcomed him and they moved together in the ancient rhythm, partners in the ancient dance. The Sing was forgotten, and the rest of the world as well.

They considered it a world well lost.

Chapter Ten

The afternoon seemed enchanted, so lost were Cat and Adam in the spell of their love. On the way to the Sing, he stopped the Blazer beneath a twisted tree not far from Peshlakai that was hidden from view on three sides by a spectacular rock formation.

"I want to make love to you here," he said, his face tender and grave.

"What, again?" she teased. "We're already late joining the others at the Enemy Way."

"Not now." He smiled, tilting her head up and looking into her eyes. "This is a very special tree," he told her softly. His voice, once again, had the lovely singsong cadence she heard in Ben's tones each day, but rarely in Adam's speech.

"This," he went on, "is the Eternity Tree. It is said that when a man and woman make love beneath this tree, they pledge their souls to each other for all the rest of time." He dropped a gentle kiss on her lips, keeping his eyes open and watchful. The way his lashes shadowed his blue eyes, the very way his brows slanted and his cheekbones curved, made him seem beautiful and vulnerable.

She touched his face, not speaking, but letting her eyes tell him her feelings.

"Catriona Frazer," he said, and the formality struck her ears strangely. "When you came here, you told me you wanted no ties. When I told Linda and George you were my wife, I saw in your face that it was too soon."

She started to speak, but he placed a finger on her lips. She sat quietly, waiting for whatever he had to say.

"One day—not now, but when you have had time to think of it—I will ask you to come here again with me." He started up the vehicle without looking at her, and Cat found it hard to think over the furious beating of her heart. She loved him, of that she had no doubt, but . . .

But what? she asked herself. She had tried to put all the obstacles and difficulties in their relationship out of her mind, but now she would be forced to examine them. And make a decision.

And even while her mind moved with half-acknowledged fear, her heart called her fool for hesitating even one moment. They drove on in silence; the mood was not strained but they were each caught up in their own thoughts. She put her head against his shoulder and he pulled her closer, curling his arm around her waist for the rest of the drive. Dusk fell over the land like a veil of gauze, but Cat didn't even notice until it was quite dark.

They came over a rise at the end of Black Mesa, a long, ancient ridge, that was the site of an enormous strip-mining operation, she could see movement in the distance. When they drew closer, a thousand people seemed to be milling about in the light from many cookfires and torches.

Adam helped her down from the Blazer, looking around and nodding at people passing by. "Perhaps my mother will be here tonight."

Cat felt a twinge of dismay. What would Beatrice Longshadow, who had given up her career as a world-famous opera singer to return to the ways of her ancestors, think of Adam living with an Anglo woman? Did she know about them?

"What's the matter?" he asked when she stood back a moment.

"Oh, nothing. Will your father be here tonight, too?"

"Hah! My mother, as all the world seems to know, lives on the reservation in the old ways. She chops her own wood and weaves her own cloth—despite a severe arthritis that developed last year, and that should receive proper medical attention. My father lives in a condo in Phoenix, complete with a microwave oven and Jacuzzi. I doubt we'll see *him* here."

"My, but you're hard to please," Cat murmured sweetly. He looked down at her. "Well"—she laughed—"it disturbs you that your mother won't take advantage of the benefits of the Anglo world, and it disturbs you that your father *does*."

Adam laughed too, but there was an undercurrent of bitterness in his voice. "I told you once before that The People are known for taking the best of differing cultures and making them their own. But one must pick and choose carefully."

Cat let the matter drop, but she was uneasy. What if Adam's ideas of what was acceptable to assimilate from the "outside world" were radically different from hers? She wished they'd stayed back at Peshlakai, warm and secure in each other's arms.

Joseph came up to them. "What took so long? Did you walk here?" He grinned widely, and Cat felt herself blushing. "Perhaps you were detained by a mountain lion."

She felt her flush deepening: She was still unused to the jocular Navaho banter, especially its frequent humorous references to sex.

They were joined by some others and Cat was quickly confused by all the introductions. She only prayed she wouldn't make some terrible gaffe. Adam kept her with him, which relieved her, for most of the women were congregated in one place while the menfolk were scattered here and there.

"Silversinger!" one thin young man called out. Cat recognized him as one of the teachers from near Cameron. "You are too ugly to walk with such a beautiful woman. You should let me walk with her, and then it will not look too bad, since I am so much better-looking."

Cat inwardly writhed with acute embarrassment, but Adam took the good-natured jesting in stride. "Good evening, Louis-Who-Falls-Off-His-Chair," he answered, and the other men laughed at the teacher's look of dismay. "I have," Adam continued, "an old goat that is as pretty as you. For two blankets and twenty horses, I will let you come to call on it!"

The old men laughed softly, but some of the younger ones roared at Adam's put-down, and a friendly scuffle ensued. If Cat had been ill-at-ease before, it was nothing to her present state.

Everywhere they went, someone had a nod or a word for Adam and a curious eye for his partner, although they hid it well with polite manners and calm faces. Still, Cat thought she could feel heads turning after they passed, and her shoulder blades prickled with the sensation of being watched. After a few minutes they heard the sounds of a lively argument nearby, and sure enough, they soon discovered Lee and Joseph going at it, hammer and tongs.

"And I told you to keep your long nose out of my business!" Cat's apprentice was saying, waving his hands for emphasis. Lee flounced off, casting sulky glances at the young man over her shoulder, and walked smack into Adam.

"What are you two hotheads fighting about now?" he exclaimed, catching her by the shoulders. Lee didn't even look at him, but kept glancing back to where Joseph stood in sullen anger.

"That man Joseph, he is too stupid for words! He almost lost his apprenticeship because of Ramona Bluewing, and look at her, flirting with that ranger from Window Rock." They followed her nod, and Cat saw a lively young Indian girl casting beguiling looks at a big, rawboned Navaho youth. Lee muttered something under her breath, and Adam laughed.

"And what is it to you if Joseph's girlfriend flirts

with others?" he asked, but Lee stalked away, leaving him to stare at her retreating back. "Well, what was that all about?" He turned to Cat.

"I'm not sure," she said slowly, "but I think my poor apprentice is about to find himself between the devil and the deep blue sea." Adam cocked his head questioningly, but Cat wouldn't say any more on the subject. Though she was glad that Lee seemed to be getting over her crush on Adam, she hated to see the girl get hurt again by developing feelings for Joseph. She sighed to herself. No one said love was easy.

As they visited with Adam's friends and his many uncles, aunts, and cousins, the security of his arm around her waist helped Cat to relax. As long as he was with her, everything would be all right.

The parts of the ceremony that she was allowed to see were fascinating. Adam translated some of the chants for her. They reminded her of some words he had sung to her only that morning:

>Far from the red land I walked,
>Far from the Home of The People.
>In the green land I found,
>A woman like a flower.
>Her, I have brought home with me,
>My lovely Heather Woman.
>Walk in Beauty.

Later Cat helped some of the women lay out the food on long wooden tables. A tall woman named Margaret Hernandez handed Cat a glass of cool liquid, and she took a grateful swallow. Whatever it was—and she suspected it was a western brand of home-distilled moonshine—it seemed to light up her veins from head to toe. Cat managed, barely, not to choke on the fiery drink, and got a nod of approval from the Indian woman.

"You will dance in the Squaw Dance?" Margaret asked her, and Cat shook her head. She didn't want to be any more conspicuous than she already was. She had developed an acute fear of making a fool of herself or, worse, blundering into some offense.

Lee came over and tugged at Cat's skirt. "The dance is starting."

"Oh, no, I couldn't."

"Oh, not for *you*," Lee explained. "It is only for the unmarried women." She pulled Cat away with her. "Old Lady Fast Horses asked me if you are growing a baby in your belly."

Cat stopped dead in her tracks. "What!"

"I just wanted you to be prepared. She'll ask you in front of everyone, so I thought I'd better warn you." Lee put her hand gently on Cat's arm. "I'm . . . I'm sorry for the way I acted when you first came to Peshlakai . . . I . . ."

Cat put her hand over the girl's. "It's okay. That was in the past."

Lee smiled up at her and then broke into a mischievous grin. "I'm going to make that stupid Joseph dance with me. I won't let him go until he gives me a lot of money." She moved away on graceful feet.

Adam joined Cat, and they laughed together as they watched the dancers. The single girls would drag a man into the cleared space to dance and link arms with them, so the partners faced in opposite directions. The girls swayed with the rhythm, but the men invariably looked bored or embarrassed. Ramona Bluewing had the tall ranger as her partner. She smiled as they danced, and Cat gazed around the circle, looking for Joseph, afraid to see his face.

But when she spotted him, she laughed and said, "What's he doing?"

"Joseph is trying to buy his way free of Lee, but she is telling him he is too cheap." Adam chuckled.

They watched until Joseph, with a resigned look on his face, finally met whatever price Lee had set. As her apprentice walked away, Cat saw him searching the bystanders for a sign of Ramona. Cat had seen the girl slip away into the shadows with the young ranger, but she wasn't about to disclose that to anyone.

Later, while she was again helping Margaret, Maria Tso joined them. As the evening wore on, she introduced Cat to many people, one of whom was Wayne Yazzie, the native physician from out Many Farms way. He was shorter than Adam and wore a white dress shirt with his jeans, unlike the other men, who were dressed in denim shirts or the velvet tunics that had been adopted from the Spanish centuries earlier. He had a long face and kind intelligent eyes.

"I hear you're from Michigan," he said, extending his hand to Cat and shaking it vigorously. "I graduated from the U of M Medical School."

Cat was excited to talk about home with someone who also knew and loved that verdant state, and they compared notes and even discovered they had some acquaintances in common. Somehow, the conversation turned to more personal things, and she found herself talking about her reactions to life on the reservation with this friendly stranger.

"Tell me," Wayne said, hooking his thumbs over his heavy silver belt. "Has Adam done anything about his hands?"

"His hands? What do you mean?"

Wayne relit his pipe. "Has he had the surgery yet? They must be giving him a lot of pain by now, if he hasn't."

Cat was struck dumb. She literally couldn't think of a word to say. When she looked up, Adam had joined them. The men exchanged greetings and Wayne reached out, taking Adam's left hand and turning it over. He looked at the palm, then traced a finger over the ridged areas that ran from wrist to the two end fingers.

"You fool." He shook his head sadly. "Silver-singer, you are a fool, indeed." He dropped the hand while Adam stared at him angrily.

"What is it?" Cat exclaimed. "I thought . . ." She turned toward Adam, but Wayne Yazzie jumped in when she paused, exasperation in his voice and sorrow in his dark eyes.

"Those ridges on his palms are from something that should have been taken care of long ago. Adam, you can't put it off any longer. I can see how your left hand is beginning to draw inward, and the circulation to your ring finger is compromised."

The expression of fury on Adam's face frightened Cat. Without a word he turned on his heel and walked away. She followed him, clutching at his arm, until they were off by themselves.

"Adam, *tell me*." She was terribly afraid.

"Wayne has a mouth like the Grand Canyon," Adam commented bitterly. "Yes, I ride horses. No, these 'calluses' aren't from holding the reins." He held his hands, palm up, and stared at them.

"There's somthing wrong with my hands." The words came out with cold formality, as if spoken by a robot. "Normally, the tendons that flex and extend move within sheaths of fiber, called fascia. For some unknown reason, sometimes the fascia grows to the tendon itself, adhering to it and eventually preventing movement. It happens to people who use their hands a lot in repetitive motions—typists, welders, grinders . . ."

Cat felt sick. "Oh, Adam, can't anything be done?" She couldn't bear to think of Adam unable to use his hands, unable to do the work he loved.

"Wayne says it can be done." He paused, taking a deep breath. "Wayne says that surgery is very successful. Wayne says if I don't have it done, I might cripple my hands." He looked off into the distance. "*Wayne says* . . . a lot." He held his hands up and gazed at them, his mouth a thin, twisted line. "But when all is said and done, they are *my* hands, not Wayne's."

"But Adam . . ." Cat began. He shook her off and disappeared into the crowd of men over by the corral. An old woman was complaining to one of the Anglo teachers about the drinking going on here and there. Not like the old days, when young folk were respectful, Cat heard. As she joined them, Lee brought over more of her numerous clan to meet Cat, and she was relieved not to be left standing alone.

As the evening lengthened, Cat kept an eye on Adam, but always from a distance. He seemed to be dipping deep in whatever the men were drinking, becoming aggressively merry and boisterous. She knew there was no sense talking to him while he was in that condition. But his hands. *His hands!* She couldn't stand to think about it. And she couldn't think of anything else.

Wayne saw her again and came over. "I'm sorry. I didn't mean to start something."

Cat faced his squarely. "I don't understand. Why won't he have the surgery when its so vitally important?"

The doctor blinked. "Is your view of Adam so much bigger than life that you can't see that he's afraid? Because that's it—he's deeply afraid that something will go wrong, that he'll never be able to work silver again. And surely you, of all people, must understand what that would mean to him."

"But is it so risky?" She wanted to hear that it was nothing, that there was no danger to her beloved Adam, but Wayne had no such reassurance for her.

"The hand is incredibly complex, Catriona. It's

an intricate and delicately structured marvel of engineering. And like any complicated piece of machinery, the more moving parts there are, the greater the possibility of malfunction. Sure, most of the surgeries I've seen on the hand have gone well. But there's always the chance of hemorrhage, or infection, or nerve damage. There are never any guarantees with surgery."

Cat twisted her hands together. "But it must be done?"

"Yes. Already early contractures are starting. His left hand is drawing up. It might stay that way for years or progress rapidly, until it's drawn up in a useless ball. And the circulation is getting constricted to those fingers. Use whatever influence you have with him to make Adam Silversinger see reason."

"I'll do what I can," she promised, but with little hope of swaying Adam. He was as stubborn in his own way as she was. Wayne nodded, and Cat left him.

She looked for Adam and found him at the front of a cheering, gesticulating crowd. A line of torches marked either side of a long, clear area. She saw two unsaddled horses prancing in excitement, and before she had time to realize what was happening, Adam and another man leaped onto the horses and rode off in swirling clouds of dust down the route staked out with the torches.

"What's going on?" she asked Joseph, who stood nearby.

He flushed to the roots of his hair and evaded her

penetrating eye. "Nothing. It's just a race. A horse race."

Cat turned toward Lee, who was hanging about the fringes of the crowd, but although she was sure Lee heard her call, the girl whirled away into the throng. Cat had the unhappy feeling that there was something going on that concerned her. Something she didn't really want to know about. Her sixth sense urged her to walk away, but her hardheadedness made her stand her ground.

In the distance, she could see the two horsemen turning back. How they rode! Like the wind itself, she thought as they came galloping back toward the crowd, each man as much a part of his horse as any centaur from the old legends. With a hail of gravel and small clods of dirt, Adam pulled his mount to a quick halt a few feet away. He jumped off the horse and accepted the congratulations of his friends while the other rider pulled up and jumped down. The two racers shook hands and Cat saw it was the teacher from out Many Farms way.

"You are one lucky devil," the man told Adam in English. Then he grinned and twitched his lips in Cat's direction, in that gesture so common among the Navaho. "No, you are *two* lucky devils!" He shook hands again and left.

"I'll bet you are glad your man won that race," the woman called Margaret told Cat from somewhere beside her. "I do not think you would like to leave Silversinger so soon!"

Cat turned and saw an amused gleam in the woman's eye, and perhaps the faintest touch of malice. "What do you mean?"

The glee on the other woman's face was obvious now. "Why, if Louis had won the race, you would have had to go home with him. *You* were the wager!"

Cat couldn't believe her ears. She was so angry she couldn't speak, couldn't even see for a dangerous moment. A red mist filled her vision. Hot words were choked in her throat by the lump of fury that threatened to constrict her breathing. She pushed past the woman rudely and went after Adam, who stood in a group of men, laughing and exchanging stories. Rage radiated from her, and the crowd divided like the Red Sea until she was face to face with him, her arms akimbo and eyes flashing fire as brightly as her hair in the torchlight.

"You bet *me* on a horse race!" The words were bitten off sharply, as if bitter to her tongue. "How dare you! How dare you!" Her hands knotted into fists to pummel his chest.

"What's the matter?" He grinned, a twinkle dancing in his blue eyes. "I *won!*"

The other men roared at the spectacle and Cat swore and beat her hands against him, but it was like hitting stone for all the effect she had.

"Perhaps it is a good thing you did." Louis laughed shaking his head, and the bystanders went off in gales of laughter again. Cat turned and was about to run away, when Adam grabbed her around the waist and lifted her right off her feet.

"It was just a joke, Small Heather Woman—a little Navaho humor!"

"Maybe I don't appreciate your 'Navaho humor,'" she snapped, trying to escape his strong grip. "Let me go. I want to go home!" she said fiercely, not as quietly as she had intended.

Adam turned to his friends. "If you will excuse me, my good uncles and cousins, I have a new wife, and as you can see, she is anxious to get home to bed." Without further ado, he tossed her over his shoulder and ambled away to where their Blazer was parked. A chorus of laughter accompanied their departure.

"You are in no condition to drive," she said through clenched teeth.

He only grinned. Opening the driver's side, he tossed her in the vehicle without further ceremony, and before she could unlock her door, Adam had started the truck and was tooling across the packed earth. He waved gaily out his window, tooted the horn, and swerved off toward the east, which Cat knew was the wrong direction.

"Stop, you fool. Go that way." She pointed vaguely in the direction from which she thought they'd come earlier.

"All right, Screeching Cat Woman." Adam laughed, still in fine fettle. He brought the Blazer around abruptly without once letting up on the gas.

Oh, well, Cat tried to calm herself, at least there's not much of anything he can run into out here. Then she remembered White Ruins Canyon and the way the gash was cut deep into the flat plain.

"Adam, let me drive. Please!"

"Okay," he said agreeably, still keeping his foot on the accelerator. The cool wind that blew through the windows seemed to quiet him down somewhat, and his driving, though erratic, didn't seem to put them in any immediate peril. Still, it seemed to Cat that they drove forever. All she wanted to do was lock herself in her room and have a good cry, and here she was, trapped in the Blazer on an endless ride. She didn't even know where they were. They might as well have been driving in circles.

It wasn't until some time later that the truth dawned on her. They *were* driving in circles. "Adam, we're lost!"

"Nonsense."

"Yes we are!" She could have almost screamed with frustration.

"Well, I thought we were back at Peshlakai, but I guess not." He turned off the engine and turned to her with a happy grin. "We'll just have to spend the night here." He took off his hat and tilted his head back against the seat. The next thing she knew, he was snoring softly.

Damn. Damn. *Damn!* She thought of trying to push him out of the way and driving on herself, but she had no idea of where they might be. In the distance a coyote howled. At least, that's what she thought it was. Damn.

She crawled between the bucket seats and lay down on the backseat cushions. The seats were cold and the temperature outside had begun to drop. Cat remembered there was a survival box in the backseat, and she dug out two heavy woolen blankets and a rug.

After a brief inner struggle, she opened one of the blankets and covered Adam from his wide shoulders to the top of his soft buckskin boots. Cat looked a moment at his strong aristocratic profile, the thin patrician nose, the firm mouth that had kissed her own so passionately a few hours before, but she remained unmoved. Clinging to her anger and outraged pride, she wrapped herself in the other blanket and pulled the rug over her.

Adam, totally insensible to the turmoil roiling through her, slept soundly. Her last thought before falling asleep was that she hoped he'd be sore and stiff as a board when he woke up.

She certainly was.

Chapter Eleven

Just before the first light of dawn, Cat awoke to an eerie world still awash in pallid moonlight where fantastical shadows played on her always vivid imagination. From the corners of her eyes, she would think she saw movement, but always a full view displayed a still and silent world. And a cold one. She reached over the front seat, groaning at her already aching muscles, and shook Adam's shoulder.

"Adam! Adam, are you asleep?"

Instantly he opened one eye, then the other. A small smile played about his mobile lips and he looked altogether too alert for a man who had seemingly had far too much to drink a few hours ago. He sat up and stretched fluidly.

"Cooled down, Cat Woman?" he asked with a flash of his white teeth in the last rays of moonlight.

Cat confronted him suspiciously. She drew herself up wrathfully. "Have you been asleep? Or was this all another one of your Navaho jokes. Where are we?"

"Well, I said we were almost to Peshlakai, but *you* said that we weren't." He bit his lower lip a moment. "And I was taught never to argue with an angry person, especially an angry woman." Then he couldn't control his mirth any longer, and that devilish grin she knew so well split his face as he laughed out loud.

"Adam, where are we?" Cat was cold and sore and furious. Her pride was bitterly hurt. He had made a laughing stock of her in front of all those people. His people. The Dinee. Even if she believed that it was just a silly joke—and she wasn't at all convinced of that—it had made her feel she would never belong. She was an outsider, set apart forever by her ways and by her very looks. Cat was from the Bellicani world, and Adam was of The People. She remembered the rest of his song he had sung for her once.

> In the green land I walk
> Far from the home of The People,
> Far from the red land I walk,
> Far from the home of The People,
> But always I return to it,
> Return to the land of my People . . .

The words echoed through her head. She didn't say another word as he started the engine. They topped the rise a few hundred yards ahead and Peshlakai was revealed below them. The angles of the buildings merged into the shadows so the school and the hogans seemed to be just one more strange sandstone formation in the predawn glow.

That was all that was needed to put Cat into a monumental rage. Not content with humiliating her at the Sing, Adam was still maliciously making fun of her. And the fact that he looked so fresh, while she felt like hell, only reinforced her rage. Tears of anger and frustration stung her eyes as the events of the night ran through her mind. When Adam brought the vehicle up outside their front door, she jumped out and hurried into the building, slamming the door shut behind her.

"Oh, come on, Cat," Adam cajoled as he pushed his way into the hallway. "What ever happened to your sense of humor?"

She ran down the hall to their bedroom and tried to slam the door, but he was right on her heels, wedging his tall frame into the opening.

"Cat! I told you the horse-race business was just a joke." Now his voice had an angry edge to it and his mouth was compressed in a thin line. "You're acting like I'm some Hollywood Indian, trading you for a string of beads or something."

He came toward her, but she turned her back and stood rigid as a poker as he touched her shoulders in the way that usually filled her with quiet pleasure. She jerked away from him, then spun around, face white with intensity. "Leave me alone."

"Cat," he said softly, and his face was suddenly contrite. She wavered for a moment, and if he'd kept his mouth shut, it might have ended there, but exasperation goaded him. "Come on, Cat, don't be so damn childish. You're acting like a—" Too late, he stopped.

That was it. "Acting like a *what?*" she said, the words dropping like stones. "Like some spoiled Bellicana? Like some spoiled Anglo woman? Well, that's what I am, at least by your way of thinking. I've never been the 'bet' in a horse race before, or the butt of some elaborate public joke. Yet *you* were the one who made a scene, slinging me over your shoulder like a sack of potatoes." She was trembling with indignation.

"Think again, Cat Woman. *You* spoke harshly to me in front of my people." His voice slashed. "I told you once before not to try and bring me to my knees with your Anglo ways." His face was now as dark as hers was white, and his brows met in one emphatic slash of black. "Remember, things are different here. This isn't suburbia with hogans or camping out for a week in the north woods. The Navaho Way is just *that*—a way of life. You won't last here unless you fit in, and you'll never fit in unless you understand that."

The words were out and the atmosphere of the room, already rife with emotion, filled with a silence louder than any sound.

"Yes," she answered at last. The cool evenness of that one word reflected her sudden and deadly calm. "Here things are only one way. *Your* way." She went to the door that led from their bedroom to the outside, but he reached it first and blocked her exit.

"What do you mean by that little remark?" he demanded angrily.

"You heard me. Everything is fine as long as we all go completely along with what you want." Suddenly, Cat was dredging up all the little hurts and frustrations of their daily life to feed her anger.

"I gave in to you about Joseph Osborne," he said, incredulous. "I lost face backing down on that issue."

"Don't be silly. You were wrong and you knew it. You don't lose face when you admit you were in error. And that was the *only* time you've compromised when we've had a difference of opinion." She headed for the door to the hallway. "You're used to having Joseph and Maria and Lee kowtow to your every whim, and you can't bear to be challenged on any decision you deign to make."

A sharp oath sounded from Adam. "You're not leaving till we get this straight, Cat Woman. This is my school, and my home, and you're always butting in. Just remember that I set the pace here. If you don't like it, you can always leave."

She turned back toward him just as he stepped forward and grasped her by the shoulders. His face was cold and hard, but she addressed her comments to the wall slightly to the right of his shoulder and never once met his eyes.

"I think that might be for the best, Silversinger," she said slowly, using his familiar Indian name for the first time. "I don't belong here. You've made that absolutely clear. I don't belong and I never will, because I can't give in to you every time there's a problem or a difference of opinion. I think that we've both made a mistake."

She didn't mean to force his hand, but she was hurt and lost in that state of rigid calmness that is really anger at its most unreasonable. Even while the words tumbled from her stiff lips, a part of her was hoping Adam would say the right thing, make the right motion of reconciliation. Her heart pounded unmercifully and her hands shook at her sides while the frightened part of her waited for him to smile that lopsided smile that never failed to melt her heart. She wanted him to take her in his arms and hold her until all her doubts and fears were assuaged. She waited. And waited.

"Well," he said at last, "I should have known better. I suppose I always knew you didn't have the guts to stick it out. Life on the reservation is just too much for poor little Catriona Frazer." His voice was soft but his words were like razors, cutting her to the quick. His long fingers dug into her flesh until she winced and looked up. "What have you been doing here these past few weeks, a sociological study in primitive ways? Or just *slumming?*"

The last words came out like the crack of a whip, and he let her go so suddenly she staggered backward. This was an Adam she didn't know. She stared at him, saw the white lines etched into his face, the hands knotted at his sides, and caught the message of fury his very posture telegraphed.

She slapped his face. "That was cowardly and unforgivable. I'm getting out of here." She grabbed her suitcase out of the wardrobe and began throwing her clothes in haphazardly.

After a moment of stunned silence, Adam followed her. "Cowardly? You're the one who's running away. How dare you call me cowardly." They glared at each other over the open suitcase, now piled high with clothes. The mark of her palm flamed on his cheek. Neither one of them would back down. They just continued to build a wall of injured pride and angry words between them.

"Yes," Cat answered, dangerously close to her snapping point. "I do call you a coward. You look down your nose at your father for choosing a softer life than yours, and you're angry and baffled by your mother's return to the Navaho Way. You set double standards in everything, and you don't even have the conviction to practice what you preach to others." She took a hasty breath and plunged on.

"You never really forgave Theresa for refusing to have surgery for her heart, and yet you're afraid to have the surgery you need so desperately on your hands! You're so afraid to take the chance of surgery that you'd rather risk being permanently crippled."

Adam gasped like a drowning man as her torrent of words flooded over him. "Why did you ever come here?" he cried out. "I wish I'd never set eyes on you!"

Cat watched his face, horrified not by his words, but by the anguish carved across his features. "Oh, Adam! I'm sorry. I didn't mean it!" She held out her hands to him, but Adam threw his arms up defensively, as if to ward off a mortal blow. She stopped, aghast, and then brushed by him quickly.

She bolted down the hall to the workroom, her eyes seeing nothing but the memory of his face, white and twisted with pain. She was sick inside. Her words and actions, as well as his, had carried things too far. And because she couldn't go back and unsay the hateful words that had brought such torment to him, because she couldn't blot out the memory, Cat did a very human thing. She made a fortress of her pride and took refuge in it.

She slammed her tool case atop the workbench, trying to calm her whirling emotions. Systematically she began placing her things inside with hands that were stiff and cold as ice. She felt as if she would never be warm again. She cleared the table of everything but the Apache Tears necklace, which lay in hundreds of unsoldered pieces on her heavy paper pattern, the intricate lines kept from distortion by hundreds of map pins. She looked at the necklace, the symbol of the love she'd shared with Adam, and blinked away the tears that threatened to spill.

"Take the necklace," Adam said, his voice sharp with a hard, cutting edge. Cat jumped. She hadn't even heard him come in the room. "Take everything of yours and get out of my life," he continued in that cool, cruel tone. "I want no reminders that you were ever here."

Cat ignored him, although his words were like blows to her stomach. Waves of ice radiated outward from deep in her soul. She felt frozen, an emotional zombie, as she methodically checked for anything she might have overlooked. She left the Apache Tears necklace behind. She had been making it as a showpiece from Peshlakai, and the stones and silver were part of the school's stock, so she wouldn't have taken it with her even if she had been able to bear the memories it represented.

Still in a state of icy calm, Cat strode over to

Joseph's work station and checked through the drawers for some special tools she had loaned him. She grabbed the wrong end of a velvet bag and a plastic tray lined with cheap imitation velvet fell to the floor.

Adam swore savagely and she watched in horror as dozens of poorly crafted pieces of Indian-style jewelry spilled out.

"This is what comes of listening to you, Cat Woman." He kicked a gaudy cigarette lighter case away with the toe of his boot. It rolled across the floor and winked accusingly at Cat in the morning sunshine, proof of her failure with her apprentice.

Then footsteps in the doorway announced that they were no longer alone. Joseph stood on the threshold, Lee right behind him.

"I'll get my things and go," he said quietly as Adam turned away in disgust. Joseph made no excuses, offered no apologies, as he began picking up the trinkets scattered on the floor. Lee knelt beside him and helped to gather the rings and bracelets and other items. Her eyes darted from Adam to Cat and back again, hopelessly. No one said a word until Joseph, head up and back straight, left the room with quiet dignity.

Then Lee flew to Adam's side, dark eyes frightened and pleading. "Silversinger, it was all the fault of that Bluewing girl. She is not a good woman, that girl, always talking of brick houses and stereos and Bellicani ways." She clung to Adam's arm. "Oh, Silversinger, Joseph is a good man and now he knows Ramona is not good for him. He did it for her, he told me, but he changed his mind last night. He promised me he would melt down all those pieces the next time you and Cat were away."

Adam brushed Lee away carelessly. The look on his face would have frozen water. "It is useless. I warned Joseph before that there was no place at Peshlakai for someone who had so little integrity, someone who would betray his heritage and his principles for money. Once, against my better judgment, I gave him another chance. You see how he has honored my trust." His voice had the finality of a steel door slamming shut. He shot a look at Cat and she was both angry and humiliated by the turn of events. The ice in her veins melted before the blaze of anger that swept through her.

"Don't waste your breath on it, Lee. It's useless to ask him for forgiveness. He doesn't know the meaning of the word."

Adam swung around on his heel and stalked out of the room, leaving the women to stare at each other.

"I've never seen him so furious," Lee whispered. "Cat, you must help Joseph." Tears brightened her dark eyes.

"I can't help him, Lee. I can't even help myself." Cat took her tool case and continued to fill it with her belongings. It took her longer to pack her gear than her clothes, and she was still at it when Joseph returned to the room.

He twisted the brim of his dark brown hat between his fingers while he addressed Lee, and although his words were halting, they carried the lilting cadence.

"Lee Chen, you have been a friend to me. Your words, they have defended me. Now I must go from this place, and my heart, it bursts with sorrow. Always, though I go far, I will remember these past months. Always I will remember my friend, Lee Chen."

The girl was either too shy or too overcome to answer. She looked down at her feet a moment, and when she looked up, her heart was in her eyes. Then in one of her quick, graceful movements, Lee turned and fled the room. Joseph turned to Cat.

"Catriona Frazer, I have learned much from you about the working of silver and the setting of stones. And you have taught me other things as well. I will not forget them." He looked older, Cat thought, the extinguished boyish enthusiasm replaced by a new maturity.

She took the hand he offered and sighed. "We've both learned a lot." She threw her shoulders back and lifted her chin. "You're a talented silversmith, Joseph. What will you do now? Where will you go?"

"I need to leave the reservation for a while. I will go to my cousin in Flagstaff, then probably to my family near Chinle later." He looked at her sadly. "Where will *you* go?"

"I want to go . . ." Where? *Anywhere*, as long as it was far from Peshlakai. And then it came to her. "I want," she said firmly, fighting back the unshed tears, "to go *home*."

Chapter Twelve

When she first returned to Michigan, Cat had no other goal than to put as much distance as possible between herself and Adam. She borrowed Mabel Walker's cabin in the northern woods and reveled in the emerald green of meadows and forests, the aqua and sapphire of the ponds and lakes that dotted the countryside. But no matter how verdant and lush the land, or how hard she tried, her eyes were filled with the beige and gray and red of the Arizona high country. And her mind was filled with thoughts of Adam.

During the day she could focus on their final arguments and convince herself that he had been arrogant and inflexible and unreasonably cruel. But at night, back in Detroit, she lay awake in the muggy heat of August, and remembered.

Sometimes the image of Adam that tormented her half-dreams was so real, so almost tangible that she could smell his familiar scent of amber and feel his touch moving lightly, teasingly, over her fevered body. Other times in her half-dreams, they would be back at White Ruins Canyon lying in each other's arms by the Morning Glory Pool, all flushed with lovemaking, and she could taste the salt of his skin as she traced it lightly with her tongue.

Then she'd waken to the sound of a passing car or the wail of a siren, and finding herself alone in her bed, she'd cry herself back to sleep.

Four weeks passed by in a haze of misery. "For God's sake, why don't you write him?" Angelica finally said one sultry morning. "If you care as much as you seem to, forget your damned pride and be the one to make the first move."

Cat poured two glasses of chilled orange juice. "You don't understand, Angel. It wasn't just a fight, a misunderstanding. We live in two separate worlds. I went to the reservation thinking it was not really going to be all that different. I know it was stupid of me." She waved aside her friend's exasperated comment. "I guess I thought the Navaho would be like any other dual-background group in America, having their own traditions and heritage with a few of the elderly or the young clinging to the old ways. I didn't even know, till I got there, that they speak in the Navaho tongue most of the time. To The People, we're still the foreigners . . ."

"I can't see why that's stopping you, if you love him, Cat," her roommate answered. But she let the matter drop for a while.

While Cat made no further comment, her restlessness and increasing sense of profound loss continued to interfere with every aspect of her life. Adam had been more than her lover; he had been companion, teacher, sometimes even child, and always her closest friend. Her other half. Only a fatal feeling that he would spurn any attempt at reconciliation had prevented her from contacting him. But Angelica's words had given Cat the last push she needed to write him. She threw away her first several attempts, then wrote a short, carefully worded note.

> Adam,
> I don't know what happened between us. I never thought it would end this way. Please believe I never meant to hurt you. I only hope you can forget the words I spoke in anger that last day.

She sat there awhile, staring at the paper. The words apologized, but they did not speak of the future. She didn't have the courage to do that, to make herself that vulnerable to his rejection. Surely he would be able to read between the lines. Surely he would take the next step and follow up on her note. If he still wanted her.

But what if he couldn't bend, couldn't change? And what if she couldn't bend enough? Did he really mean all he'd said to her the day they parted? Did he really see her as a silly, spoiled Bellicana who could never, ever fit into his chosen way of life?

The thought was too painful, and she put it aside. She picked up her pen and finished the letter.

> Remember me to Maria and Lee and Ben Slowhorse, and thank them for their kindness.

She wanted to add more, but pride and fear of appearing foolish prevented it. She signed it simply, Cat.

She watched the mailbox every day for the next three weeks, waiting for his answer. Waiting and hoping for a letter that never came.

She immersed herself in preparation for a coming show, and all her grief and loneliness were transmitted into her creations, so that each piece of silver worked by her hands became alive with emotion. Cat found herself using stones she'd never liked before, and was particularly drawn to polished agate and picture jasper. They reminded her of the subtle colors of the desert and the high country of the reservation that she had never fully appreciated. And they reminded her of Adam, who was sprung from the arid soil, as much a part of his land as the stark, invincible rock. As the warm September and October days of Indian Summer painted the trees in the shimmering golds and greens and yellows she had been so homesick for, she found that even her perception of colors had been altered. The landscape around her seemed almost garish in its bright shades and high contrasts, as if someone had spilled jars of clashing colors over everything. Then late one afternoon, there was a knock on her door.

Cat replaced her soldering iron and wiped her hands against the legs of her jeans. Probably the paperboy, she thought. But when she opened the door she had a surprise.

The woman on the doorstep was tall, elegantly

thin, and dressed in the height of fashion. She could have been any matron from Grosse Pointe or New York or Palm Springs, but Cat wasn't fooled. She'd seen her picture only once or twice, but the high cheekbones, aristocratic nose, and wide, thin lips were unmistakable. And so were the eyes, dark blue and startling in the bronze skin.

Cat gestured, holding the door wider, and the visitor stepped inside.

"You *are* Catriona Frazer," she said, and it wasn't a question. She introduced herself, but it was unnecessary. "I am Adam's mother, Beatrice Longshadow."

Cat invited her to sit down and abstractedly made them some instant iced tea. What was Beatrice Longshadow doing in Michigan? Cat remembered that Adam's mother rarely left the reservation. Perhaps he had sent her. The thought made her heart thud against her ribs.

"Adam persuaded me to leave the reservation to help the Arthritis Foundation," the woman said in a rich contralto. "We'll be doing a benefit with the Detroit Symphony Orchestra." That explained her presence in Michigan.

But what does a benefit with the DSO have to do with me? Cat wondered. And hoped.

Beatrice Longshadow eyed Cat thoughtfully. "I was asked to bring you a message."

Cat's palms were sweaty as she waited to hear the message that meant so much to her. She leaned forward.

"George and Linda Gerisch want me to remind

you of your promise; their show in Sedona is next week, and they are counting on your presence. I was to tell you that the gentleman from Texas is coming specifically to meet you, and Linda is sure he has a commission in mind."

Cat's heart sank. She'd heard from the Texan, Jonas Brown, and she knew the trip would be well worth it, both financially and as an enhancement of her reputation. Six weeks ago she would have been ecstatic at the opportunity. Now she barely assimilated the message. It wasn't what she'd been hoping to hear.

Beatrice Longshadow looked at her keenly, and her gaze, so much like Adam's, pierced Cat to the heart. "I think I have another message for you," the woman said. "This time from me." She rose gracefully despite a small line of pain that formed between her eyes with the movement.

Cat stood too.

"I see," the older woman continued, "that you are a proud woman. My son, he is a proud man. And very foolish." She took one of Cat's hands in her own, the once shapely fingers distorted by her swollen joints. "Go to him, Catriona Frazer. He needs you. He needs you, but he will never ask . . ." Beatrice Longshadow dropped Cat's hand and reached into the heavy canvas bag she'd brought with her. "These belong to you." Without another word, she took out a long box and placed it in Cat's hands. Then she was gone, moving with the same silent grace her son had inherited.

Cat sat down slowly, then lifted the lid. Inside,

under layers of cotton, she uncovered the mountain-lion necklace Adam had made for her and the matching belt. She touched the cool silver and remembered the touch of Adam's hands, gliding over her skin; she clasped the necklace behind her neck, and as it fell along her breasts, she remembered the touch of his mouth upon them and she was shaken with a wild longing for him. She wanted him, wanted to feel the warmth of his body on hers, wanted him joined to her in the intimacy of love, exorcising the terrible loneliness and fear she felt. Her need for Adam was more than physical longing. She desperately needed the sense of completeness he had brought to her life, the fulfillment she had known sharing each day with him.

With fingers that shook, she rifled through the cotton, but there was no letter, no note, not even one line with his name. And no jacia earrings. If they had been there, she thought in anguish, she would know that he still cared and that there was some hope they could work things out. But there were no green jacia earrings and there was no note. He doesn't love me. Or he doesn't love me enough!

Then she remembered Beatrice's words. "He needs you. He needs you, but he will never ask . . ." What kind of love is that? she thought. I wrote to him and he never even bothered to answer. I swallowed my pride—at least a little. Why can't he? She closed her eyes. Her thoughts were too confused; she couldn't even begin to sort them out.

When Angelica came home an hour later with Mabel Walker in tow, Cat was still sitting in the living room, the silver necklace draped around her neck and the belt lying in her hands.

"Cat, those are fabulous," Mabel exclaimed as Angelica went to her room to change. Startled, Cat held the belt out for the gallery owner to examine. "I thought these were your work, at first glance," she told Cat as she turned the belt over and read Adam's name stamped on the back. "But there's a more masculine strength behind these pieces, as I see from the silversmith's mark." She handed the belt back to Cat, and although her voice was brisk, her faded eyes showed a real concern. "When you left for Arizona with Adam Hawk, I really thought you'd never be back again, except for an occasional show." She placed a beringed hand on Cat's arm. "What happened in Arizona, dear?"

Cat poured out her story, and a torrent of tears as well, as her defenses fell in the face of her old friend's sympathetic concern. Mabel listened to the jumble of pride and anger and love, and let Cat finish both her recital and her tears before speaking.

"What you're saying is that you do love him but you're not sure of how much he loves you." She brushed a damp curl away from Cat's forehead. "Catriona, dear, you never knew my first husband, Karl Blane, the sculptor. I was crazy about him."

Her eyes were dreamy a moment as she looked backward in time.

"Well, Cat, I realized right at the beginning that Karl loved me as much as he was able. It wasn't as much as I wanted, but I knew he couldn't love me any more than he did." Her voice softened. "And no matter how I tried, I couldn't love him any less."

Mabel's words did nothing to soothe Cat's mind; she understood what her friend meant, but that wasn't what Cat wanted with Adam. No, she yearned for a loving relationship that was worked at and cherished by both partners. She wanted him to feel as deeply as she did. But what if he wasn't able to give that much? Or what if he was unable to show it?

That night Cat nearly drove herself crazy trying to come to a decision. If Adam really needed her, really loved her, why couldn't he let her know? Was it some basic cultural principle or some emotional barrier that prevented him from doing so? But Beatrice hadn't said that Adam *loved* her. She had said "Adam needs you," and that might be an altogether different thing.

For a while it seemed that Cat's fears and stubborn Scot's pride were bigger than her love for Adam and her longing for the comfort of his arms. But pride is a lonely bedmate, and when she finally fell asleep shortly before dawn, Cat had made up her mind.

She'd go to Sedona for the show. Adam would have to be there for it, too. After that, it would be up to him. If he could meet her halfway—perhaps even less than halfway— There was no sense in thinking any further. She'd go to Sedona and see what happened.

Cat rolled over and for the first time in weeks drifted into a deep and blissfully refreshing sleep.

Chapter Thirteen

The morning of the show in Sedona, Cat woke too early. This is it, she thought, today I'll see Adam. Today I'll know if there's anything left between us. Pulling back the curtains in her room at the Cedar Motel, she watched the dawn glow as it lit the red and gold spires of Oak Creek Canyon. Cat opened the door and stepped out on the balcony, inhaling deeply the heady scents of cedar and juniper that filled the air. The hum of insects rose from the creek.

Suddenly she was homesick, but not for the green freshness of her Michigan. No, her eyes longed for the wide open reaches of the reservation, the subtle gray to rose shadings of the eerily beautiful Painted Desert, the majestic buttes and needles of rock that kept watch over the moonscape of Monument Valley. And the warm, blue waters of the Morning Glory Pool in White Ruins Canyon, where she and Adam had splashed and made love.

She remembered his tall, hard body, all glistening bronze in the sunlight, and the ripple of his muscles and and tendons as he moved. At the very thought of him her nipples tightened beneath the silky gown and her nerves tingled with the memory of his touch. If by some magic Adam had walked into the room, she would have done anything in her power to seduce him into her arms. Yet, despite the way her body ached for him, coming back to Arizona had also been a decision of heart and mind. The closer she had come to Adam's country, the more Cat knew that this was what she wanted, that this was where she belonged. But only with him.

As she dressed, she was in such a state of nervousness that her stomach seemed continually knotted, and she wondered if her heart would ever slow to a normal rate again. She chose a dress of sheer white cotton from India embroidered with white floss. After a severe inner struggle, she pulled the belt Adam had made for her from the overnight case.

Slowly she fingered each smooth oval, and the flashes of morning light made the stylized mountain lions seem to move lithely beneath her touch. She clasped the belt around her waist, remembering the way Adam had once placed it there for her. She had to wear it. Surely one look at her wearing his gift of love would tell Adam how she felt about him.

She twisted her hair up in a knot at the nape of her neck, the way she always wore it while working. She thought of how he would always come up behind her and kiss her just behind the ear. And if no one was around, he'd pull loose the pins and let her hair tumble down about her shoulders, tangling his hands in the silken snare, burying his face in it.

Now, preparing to face him after their bitter parting, Cat was determined to do everything she could to make him remember. Make him want her again.

Maybe it couldn't be done, but Catriona Frazer was going to do her damnedest.

When she arrived, George and Linda's shop in Tlaquepaque was packed with throngs of tourists and buyers and people who lived in the area. The preliminary judging had taken place privately the evening before, but Cat had gotten in late. Besides, she wanted to blend into the crowd when she entered the shop. She wanted to get her bearings before coming face to face with Adam.

"Catriona!" It was George, coming around a clump of people bent over a long display case. He gave her one of his big bear hugs, lifting her completely off her feet.

"Put her down, George, before you crush her." Linda laughed, joining them. "Did you know your bracelets won a second place?" she added.

She led Cat through the throng to the back wall of the room where, spotlighted in a case by themselves, her two bracelets were arranged on black velvet. Below her name, Cat saw the green ribbon. She'd hoped for a first place, but all in all she was pleased. Her work was good, and the judges had recognized it.

One of the bracelets was a thin spiraling curve made to fit a woman's upper arm, all bright line and shape like an elegantly sensuous snake. The second one, Cat's favorite, was a man's bracelet. She had fashioned it in the Hopi overlay method, bonding the top sheet with its cutout geometric designs to a lower sheet of silver so that it appeared to be carved from one smooth block. Then, in a departure from traditional Hopi style, she had taken a polished oval of beige and tan picture jasper, laced with a black marking in the shape of a twisted tree, and set it in the center. It was boldly designed and cleverly executed. And all the time she had been making it, she had thought of Adam and the Eternity Tree.

"Here's another one that you'll be proud of," George said, indicating a wall display. In the glass case that hung over a yellow third-place ribbon, she saw a pair of matching men's cuff bracelets. They blazed with hundreds of pieces of inset coral, one gleaming with the stair-step cloud symbol in white shell, the other slashed by a zigzag lightning symbol in gold. Cat knew it must have taken many, many hours to set each tiny facet of stone so precisely, and she glanced at the card to see the smith's name.

In black letters it read simply, JOSEPH OSBORNE, PESHLAKAI. A brown hand descended on her shoulder and she turned to find her former apprentice beaming at her.

"Welcome back, Catriona Frazer. It is good to see you here." He paused and looked at her carefully. "Are you here to stay?"

She mumbled something, but then she couldn't help herself and blurted out the question most on her mind. "Is Adam Silversinger here?" Somehow the two names came out together, as if even in her own mind they belonged that way.

Joseph shifted his weight from one foot to the

other. "No. Silversinger does not leave the reservation . . . anymore." He looked acutely uncomfortable and Cat couldn't understand why.

"Have you seen him since . . . since we left?" she asked in a small voice.

The young man looked surprised. "Yes. I went back to Peshlakai three weeks later."

Now it was Cat's turn to be surprised. "And Adam took you back?"

"Not exactly. He contacted me in Flagstaff. He *asked* me to come back." Someone hailed the young silversmith and he excused himself, promising to return.

She was glad to be alone, swallowed up in the crowd, so that no one saw the tears stinging her eyes. She ducked past a couple of teenagers and fled out into the sunshine.

Adam had asked Joseph to come back, but had never even answered her letter. She found a tiny court between the sides of two buildings and took refuge from the sun in the shade of an ancient sycamore. No one passed by and only the stone gargoyle on the tiled fountain facing Cat saw her tears.

Her determination faltered and fell beneath a fresh onslaught of doubts. In her mind, she had drawn a picture of Adam lost and lonely, prevented only by his proud self-sufficiency from reaching out to her. Now she saw it was a faulty portrait, colored by her own wishful thinking.

"I was stupid to come back to Arizona," she whispered fiercely. "He doesn't care. He's not even here. I came all this way to see him, just to see if we could still work things out, and he couldn't even come a few hundred miles." Well, the trip wasn't a wasted effort. She had taken second place, and Linda had arranged an appointment for her with the Texan. Oh, God! What time was it?

Cat straightened out her skirt and smoothed the tendrils escaping from her chignon. She hoped she looked presentable as she hurried back to the shop.

It was lunchtime and the crowd had thinned out to a few idly curious tourists. Linda took one look at Cat's pale face and hustled her into the office. "You look like you've been hit by a truck. Are you all right?"

"Just too much sun," Cat lied politely.

Linda forced her out to lunch at the Mexican restaurant near the back of Tlaquepaque and the light meal made her feel more human. They were back in Linda's shop in half an hour.

The Texan came in just then. He was a tall, blond man in a khaki shirt and slacks. He had a tanned, pleasant face and a slow, lazy drawl that made Cat want to finish all his sentences for him. He purchased a necklace and several rings that Cat had placed on consignment with George and Linda, and was determined to have the two prize-winning bracelets when the show closed.

"I want that arm bracelet for my daughter. It'd look mighty fine on her." He opened his wallet again and pulled out a picture of a shy-looking, dark-haired girl with an oval face and a smooth, olive-toned complexion. Cat had to admit the silver spiral would be set off perfectly by the girl's skin, but she didn't want to sell the piece just yet.

"Well, you'll let me buy the jasper bracelet, though, won't you, ma'am?"

Sell the jasper piece? But that was Adam's bracelet! No one else could ever wear it, Cat thought.

They compromised at last, the Texan offering almost twice what Cat had wanted to part with the woman's silver bangle, but she remained adamant on the other piece. She had made the Eternity Bracelet with Adam in mind, and if he never wore it, well, neither would anyone else. The Texan commissioned some pieces from Cat, things that she had swiftly sketched according to his rather hazy ideas, and he was delighted with her ability to capture his thoughts.

He left, and for the first time Cat was alone in the showroom. She wandered the aisles, looking at the other pieces while Linda handled some business in her office. Rounding a small pillar, Cat received a shock.

There before her was a necklace. *Her* necklace. The intricate lines of minute silver beads radiated outward over a background of palest peach velvet and the Apache Tears hung from their settings like dark drops of raw honey, sable with amber hearts where the light struck through.

Cat moved closer. Her necklace, and yet not really hers, for there were many subtle differences within the design as well as in the craftsmanship of the piece. Where she had used all polished tubes of silver, the maker had randomly replaced at least half of them with bark-textured beads, scattering a few copper rectangles about for warmth. And where

Cat had planned small teardrop pieces of the brown-black obsidian, the smith who made this necklace had used larger, more irregular shapes. And it worked. Oh, how it worked!

The longer she looked at the beautiful collar of silver and Apache Tears, the more she realized it was not really the necklace she had designed at all. No, this was truly a masterpiece, using light and shadow as part of the design, gaining vitality from the controlled use of silver and copper, and drawing strength and potency from the primitive natural shapes of the glassy stones.

When she at last dragged her eyes away from the stunning beauty of the Apache Tears necklace, Cat was not surprised by the blue ribbon of the first-place award, or the white special-prize ribbon pinned beneath the display. Nor was she surprised to see the name ADAM SILVERSINGER on the card below.

The power of the necklace and its associations started a whirlpool of emotions swirling through Catriona's brain. She didn't even hear the door open or the entrance of two newcomers until they were right beside her. Even then the words didn't register at once.

". . . yes, and all the more wonderful that he could make something so complicated and do it so well," an Indian girl in jeans and a sport shirt said.

"It's a terrible tragedy about his hands," the man with her answered.

So, Cat thought with a sick feeling, his hands have gotten worse. Oh, Adam, Adam! How can you be so foolish? How can you take such chances? Was that why you didn't answer my letter?

"Well," the girl said, "I still don't see how he could do it. Joseph Osborne said he really has the use of only one hand now . . ." Her voice trailed off as they moved to another display case and Cat stood there, numb and drained, staring at the Apache Tears necklace.

She stood there so lost in misery that she didn't hear the door open and close several more times. When she turned blindly, the shop was rapidly filling with after-lunch shoppers, and George was back behind the counter.

"Cat!" She turned around to see Joseph Osborne coming toward her with Lee on his arm. Both were smiling brightly. She accepted the girl's congratulations, but her mind was not on the prize she'd been given.

"I've just heard about Adam's hands . . ." she said, and her voice broke.

"I wanted to talk to you about that," Joseph said. "When I came back looking for you this morning, no one knew where you'd disappeared to."

"How bad are his hands?"

"Well," Lee said hesitantly, "he had the left one done first, because it was the worst, and everything went fine. And when he went back to have the other one done, it seemed like it would work out okay too."

What is she saying? Cat wondered. There was a strange roaring in her ears, and the words didn't seem to make much sense.

"To make a long story short," Joseph interjected when Lee suddenly ran out of words, "Adam got an infection in his hand after the second surgery."

"Surgery?"

"He had it done right after you went away."

"What's wrong with his hand?" Cat twisted the fabric of her skirt between fingers.

Joseph sighed. "His right hand is bad, Cat. I mean, he can use it, but the motion is very limited. He can hold things, but not pick up little pieces or use it to do fine work anymore."

"Oh, God! Is it permanent? Can't they do anything?" She was crying now, oblivious to the curious faces turned her way.

"I don't know. He doesn't talk about it," the young man said.

"He doesn't talk about much of anything, now," Lee threw in.

They guided Cat outside and along an arcade until they found a place to talk that was more private. Cat gulped some air and got herself under control outwardly, but inside, she was dying. She had taunted him. She had called him a coward and he had gone ahead with the surgery. And he had effectively lost the use of his right hand, at least as far as his silversmithing went. She dried her eyes and faced her companions.

"It's all my fault."

"Don't be silly," Joseph said crisply, suddenly sounding many years her senior. "Did you make him put off going to see Wayne Yazzie for several days when the swelling got worse? Was it your doing that the infection was resistant to the antibiotics? That was between Adam and the gods. It had nothing to do with you. And he still made that wonderful necklace, didn't he? Sure, it took him longer than it would have before. But everything that has happened to him goes into his work. Good, bad, funny, or tragic, it all shows in his work.

"I think that's why the Apache Tears necklace is a masterpiece. He loves you, Catriona Frazer. When you left, you took a part of him away. That, too, is in the necklace. That piece of jewelry is his love song to you. The only harm you did to Adam Silversinger was when you left him, Cat. But you can make it up to him if you go back."

"But does he want me back?" Her heart leaped at the thought.

Then Joseph grinned at her. "When I was leaving for Sedona yesterday, Silversinger asked me to look around; he needs another journeyman to teach at Peshlakai. He even suggested I might find out the background of the prizewinners and ask if they might be interested in working with us."

Cat lifted her chin and smiled. "Do you think that includes me?"

"Well." Her former apprentice smiled back. "He never said it didn't."

Cat went back to the shop for her purse and after giving a hasty explanation to Linda, she left for the motel to make her arrangements.

Cat had gone through so many emotions in the past few hours that she felt drained, but she was sure of one thing: Adam had loved her once, and if any spark of that love remained, she would fan the flame until it roared to life. Even if she were burned in the resulting blaze.

Chapter Fourteen

Two hours later Cat was on her way to the reservation in a light plane she'd chartered in Sedona. The sale of the silver bracelet would more than pay for the flight and she could reach Peshlakai in a few short minutes instead of after a bumpy five- or six-hour drive. Besides that, Cat thought if she arrived by car, Adam could too easily tell her to turn right around and leave. This way, she could tell the pilot to take off again immediately. Adam would have to face her.

High above Flagstaff, there was already snow on the San Francisco Peaks, which were sacred to both the Navaho and Hopi tribes. Adam had told her that the rain gods lived there and the Hopi Kachinas. There was not a moment now when he was out of her thoughts and everything she saw as they flew over the reservation brought back some special memory.

As the plane made its final approach to the poorly surfaced strip—really more of an emergency landing site and rarely used—Cat's hands were clenched tightly, her face pale in the late-afternoon sunshine. When the aircraft took off again, she was on the rise overlooking the hogans of Peshlakai.

No sign of life was evident as she descended the slope. Perhaps Adam is watching, she thought. Perhaps he's right there, by the window in front. Does he recognize me? What will he say?

But when she reached the building that housed the workshops, no one was about. Cautiously she swung the heavy door inward. The main room was empty and the kitchen strangely silent, with no pot bubbling on the back of the monstrous old stove. Maybe they're all at a Sing somewhere, she decided dejectedly.

Some impulse made her follow the short hall to her old bedroom, but when she reached the door, Cat froze for a moment, wondering what awaited her there. She pushed the door open. The room was unchanged, the oak cupboard and leather chair in their accustomed places, but the big bed was stripped bare and covered with a torn sheet. She went back out to the hall.

A faint pinging sound came from the silversmith's workroom, and she followed it down the longer hall. Ben Slowhorse was bent over his table exactly as she'd seen him that first day. He was tapping the bezel in place on something in his vise, but though she was quiet, he put his tools down and turned toward the door.

"I was worried about you," he said, peering in her direction with eyes that were now blank with blindness. "I thought you would be home much earlier."

At first Cat didn't know what to say. "It's *me*, Ben. It's Cat" she said, suddenly shy.

"Of course," the old man answered. "I know your footsteps, Catriona Frazer. And I have been listening for them too long." He tapped at the piece a few more times while she hovered in the doorway. *Home*, he had said to her.

"Come and see what I am making," he suggested.

She went forward, still hesitant of her welcome. He was working on a bow guard for a man's wrist set with rough chunks of Lander Blue turquoise, almost black with its intricate spiderwebbing of matrix. Cat sucked in a deep breath of appreciation. Ben couldn't see, but that hadn't stopped his creative genius. The craggy gemstones were set perfectly in the mirror-bright silver, a powerful statement of the artist's ability.

"That is the best piece of your work I have ever seen, Ben Slowhorse," she told him truthfully.

"For everything we lose in this world, we gain something, Catriona Frazer. I am content."

"How . . . how is Silversinger," she asked through lips that felt stiff and parched.

"It is worse than when Theresa died." Ben touched the talisman pouch hanging from his belt. "It is like there has been another death."

"Where is he?"

"When he is not working silver, sometimes he goes to White Ruins Canyon, where I took him when he was a boy. Sometimes I do not know where he goes. Other times, he walks to the tree by Three-Sided Rock and sits there."

"Thank you, Ben." She hurried out and brought her two suitcases in. Without hesitation, she carried them to the bedroom and put her things away. She found sheets in the cupboard, the blanket folded beneath, and made up the bed.

Now let him try to throw her out!

She changed into the red full-length Navaho skirt and white blouse she'd worn to the Sing at the Bluewings' hogans, and brushed her hair until it glittered like red gold. On her feet she put soft leather boots and around her waist she draped the beautiful silver belt Adam had made. She placed several bracelets around her wrists and lifted the heavy mountain-lion necklace over her hair, draping it across her breasts. She needed earrings to complete her look. Cat thought of the jacia earrings and all they symbolized. She left her earlobes bare.

She felt like a bride facing her bridegroom for the first time and she wondered what kind of reception he would give her. Her greatest hope was that he'd welcome her into his arms; her greatest fear that he'd angrily refuse to even look at her or speak to her. But for either, or anything in between, she was bound and determined to stand her ground. She wouldn't leave unless she was *sure* he no longer returned her love.

And really, what proof did she have that he did? Not a word from him all the time she had been gone. Only the box his mother had delivered. She was getting cold feet as she thought of it. Joseph and Lee thought he loved her. Beatrice Longshadow had said Adam needed her. But what did anyone else really know about the heart of another?

Fear and anticipation ran hot and cold through

her veins. It was time. She glanced in the mirror and was happily surprised by the way her face had been transformed, as if she were glowing from within.

She dabbed perfume at her pulse points, especially between her breasts where he liked it, and she was ready. The sun would be going down soon and the temperature would drop greatly. She took her long, woolen cape of dark blue, lined in heavy satin, and threw it over one arm.

The brisk walk warmed her and she went along the smooth bottom of the wash. As she neared Three-Sided Rock, she saw Adam. He was sitting on a broken slab of limestone, his shirt lying near his booted feet. Cat couldn't tell if he saw her at first, but it seemed as if the painful beating of her heart could be heard for miles. She slipped on a pebble going up the incline and he turned his head her way. She felt his blue eyes raking her from head to toe, and her foot slid in the loose soil, but she righted herself without a mishap. He didn't move, didn't speak until she finally reached him. Then Adam looked away and hurled a shard of rock down the sides of the wash. He ignored Cat's presence as if she were invisible.

Anger would have been easier to take than indifference, and her stomach knotted. Cat knew she had her work cut out for her. She watched his stern profile and noted the changes in him she had not seen at first.

He was thinner, but it suited him. And surely

those were new lines etched at the corners of his eyes. A bright red cotton headband went around his forehead and was tied in back. His raven hair was longer, almost touching his shoulders in the old style of the Navaho Way. It made him look different, older and slightly alien. And so handsome it almost broke her heart. She wanted to kneel down beside him and press his darkly chiseled face against her breasts. She wanted to feel his warm, firm mouth on hers, feel it moving down the curve of her throat, seeking the peaks of her nipples that strained now against the thin cotton of her blouse.

But that would be the wrong move now. She waited silently.

"What are you doing here?" The words came out viciously, torn from deep inside him.

Cat sat down beside him. "How are you, Adam?" Had he noticed the jewelry she wore? Silence drew out between them. She could smell the familiar amber scent of him, and it was torture to sit so quietly when his bare forearm was inches away from hers. She imagined she could feel the heat radiating from it. Her eyes traveled down the length of his thigh, and she remembered the way her fingers had moved over his skin and the way it felt to have him pressed against her. The yearning to put her arms around him, to kiss and touch and make love with him became a physical ache.

Turnabout was fair play. She leaned forward so that she brushed his arm lightly, reveling in the sensation of the touch. He jumped away as if burned, but as he rose to his feet, she saw with triumph the dark flush of desire that spread across his high cheekbones. She stood too.

"What are you doing here?" he demanded again. His eyes flew to her face and then his glance flickered over her body briefly before he looked off into the distance.

"Joseph said you were looking for a teacher. I came to ask for the job."

An oath escaped him and he spun around to face her, grasping her arms above the elbows so that the bracelet on the left one dug into her flesh.

"Go away. You're not wanted here." The words that came so readily to his lips were at complete variance with the look in his eyes, and her heart lifted.

"Are you afraid of me, Silversinger?" she asked softly, leaning forward until her thighs met his. Instantly, without warning, she was a prisoner of his hard embrace and Adam's lips came down crushingly on hers.

"Is this what you want, Heather Woman?" he asked roughly when he lifted his head. She was breathless and dizzy. He'd turned the tables on her and Cat found herself unable to speak a single coherent word. Ruthlessly his mouth was on hers again, and when she opened hers to gasp, his tongue slipped inside, twining about expertly and exploring against her will.

He bent her back over one forearm while his hand found the neck of her blouse and ripped it open, freeing her breasts for the probing of his relentless fingers. He took one of the taut buds in his fingers and rolled the rosy floret between them while his tongue ravished her mouth.

Even while part of her mind cried out that this savage plunderer was not the Adam she knew and loved, her traitorous body responded. And even in his angry passion, he seemed to remember every inch of her body, every intimate touch that drove her wild with desire. He lifted her, and before she could catch her breath, he had lowered her to the ground. She realized that the red skirt was up around her waist and nothing covered her throbbing breasts but the silver necklace and his kisses.

She offered no resistance as his lips moved over her, tantalizing each ripe nipple with teeth and tongue. The moist warmth of his mouth contrasted with the cool air in a maddeningly sensual counterpoint, and she kissed his temple, tasting his skin with her tongue.

Adam's lips grazed along her skin, moving down her body all the way to her feet, as he removed her soft suede footwear. Then slowly he moved back up, lighting fires with the soft touch of his mouth in a hundred different places. Cat slid her hands up and down his arms and her fingernails dug into his shoulders. In seconds his clothes were off, but Cat protested even that brief loss of contact. Adam looked down at her, his eyes dark as sapphires with something she couldn't interpret.

"Is this why you came back, Cat?" he asked hoarsely. She twined her arms around his neck and pulled him down against her, writhing beneath him, nipping at his chest sharply with her small, white teeth.

"Oh, Adam," she cried involuntarily. She had waited so long for this, to be with him, to make love with him. Slowly, insistently, his fingers caressed the sensitive flesh of her inner thigh and his knee urged her legs apart. She grasped at his hips, pulling him tightly against her, feeling the immediacy of his need for her and rejoicing in it.

His fingers moved beneath the elastic at her leg, sending hot showers of sparks along Cat's nerve endings, and she strained upward for his touch, shuddering with the force of her mounting passion. She pulled at the fabric, trying to tear away the last barrier to their union, and a soft moaning escaped her as Adam slid the panties over the curve of her hips and down.

She reached out for him and Adam lowered himself upon her, covering her naked body with his own. His skin seemed to burn against her like molten bronze. She felt her body melting into his.

He kissed her again; yet, in spite of her physical readiness for the final act of love, something was missing. Something very important. As his tongue probed the recesses of her mouth and his hands roved over her, exciting every cell in her body, Cat realized what it was: there was no tenderness in his kiss, no love in his passionate touching. Adam's mouth moved roughly on hers and the hands that touched her, she knew, were driven by anger and lust, not love.

She was frightened, and she struggled, pushing

her hands against his chest. He was too strong; she couldn't budge him. She beat her fists on his arms and against his back, but he held her in arms like bars of steel. She could hardly breathe and the silver necklace cut into her breasts. Anger and sorrow flooded through her, washing away all physical craving for his body to be one with hers.

Unable to put up an effective struggle, Cat lay still in his arms, then, neither fighting nor returning his caresses. It took a minute for Adam to realize the change in her, and when he did, he tried to rekindle her excitement, trailing his tongue along the line of her jaw and down to her breast. He teased a nipple with his lips, but there was only an automatic physical response in her at first. He nibbled and licked at the trembling peak as if it were a delectable morsel, and to her dismay, Cat found her arms moving up to embrace him, her legs moving apart to welcome the imminent invasion.

Everything was wrong. It was all spoiled. Her body and her own arrogance had betrayed her. And Adam's hatred. That must be what he felt; why else would he persist when it was no longer good between them? Tears silently welled in her eyes, spilling down her cheeks in hot, salty trails, and she lay still, awaiting the death of all her dreams.

Seeing her tears, Adam lifted his head and stared down at her. She read in his face anger and lust, and something that looked like pain.

"I thought this is what you came here for. Why did you change your mind, Cat?" The sneer in his voice didn't quite reach his eyes.

Cat lay on her back, unmoving. She closed her eyes against the hot tears that welled up behind her lids.

"Oh, for God's sake, Cat." Adam stood up and began putting on his jeans. When she still didn't move, he picked up her cloak and threw it at her. The blue wool covered her legs and hips, leaving her arms and breasts bare and startlingly white in contrast.

She sat up, her long, red hair swinging over her shoulder in an innocently seductive manner, and Adam swore under his breath.

Cat stood, pulling her skirt down again beneath the camouflage of the cape. There wasn't enough left of her pants or blouse to bother about, and with a proud, defiant look she threw the cloak over her shoulders. She began walking back to the cluster of buildings that were Peshlakai, head high.

Adam sprinted up behind her and whirled her about. The agony in his eyes mirrored the feelings in her own heart. He caught her in his arms, holding her so tightly she felt her bones would break. The wind caught her hair and it fluttered like ribbons over their shoulders while Adam's embrace tightened and his breath came in ragged gasps.

Then he released her abruptly and threw his hands up. "I don't know what to say. Damn it, Cat, I don't understand. At least tell me why you came here, if you don't want me."

She looked at him, saw the new lines chiseled in his face, the dark shadows beneath his eyes. "I did want you, Adam. But not like that. I wanted you with love and tenderness and all the silly little jokes we had together. I wanted you as a part of my life, not just for a moment of heated passion. But you see, I didn't know you hated me . . ." Her words trailed off.

She reached out and took his hands. He offered no resistance as she turned them over, looking at the three fine lines of pink scar tissue that radiated on each, from the wrists to the base of the fingers. She'd expected his injured hand to look different somehow, but the damage to the tendons showed no signs that her untrained eye could see. She looked back up into his eyes.

"I love you, Adam. I think I'll always love you."

He made some sound and came closer, but she pressed a finger to his mouth.

"Don't say anything. There's no need." She looked down a moment. "I came here to stay with you, work by your side. Even sleep in your bed, if you still wanted me there. At the very least I thought we could work together. And I thought it would be enough for me, just to love you. I really did. But it's not. I can't live day by day with a man who hates me." She kissed his hand tenderly, then turned and ran off toward the wash.

She hadn't gone ten feet when he caught her, sweeping her up in his strong arms.

"Oh, Cat, I can't lose you again! I do love you—so much, that when you left, it was like the sun disappeared from the sky. Don't leave me again. Don't ever leave me."

Cat saw the yearning in his eyes and her arms

wound around his neck as Adam scooped her up. He carried her back to Three-Sided Rock, then slowly stood her on her feet, letting her soft body slide down the hard muscles of his thighs.

Adam's lips were on hers again, this time brushing lightly against the softness of her mouth while he murmured words of endearment. He fumbled at the strings of her cloak, and Cat realized then how much use of his hand he had lost. Again, she took his palm and kissed it, mingling her breath and her tears against the fading red lines.

He slid his arms around her inside the cape, running his hands lightly over her bare skin, sending a rush of exquisite pleasure through her body as he stroked her curves and contours. She felt the catch of her skirt release, and the garment fell around her ankles like the petals of a fallen flower. She stepped out of it and lifted the sides of the cloak, draping them over Adam's shoulders so they were inside the tent of the cape, her breasts softly pressing against his naked chest as they stood beneath the Eternity Tree.

She raised her hands, stroking them over his chest in slow, sensual movements and he grasped her hips and brought them hard against his, graphically telegraphing his state of high arousal. Cat closed her eyes, letting her sensitive fingertips slide over the muscles of his wide shoulders and down the steel sinews of his arms. There was no hurry now. They could take all the time in the world to tease and tantalize and bring each other to the fullness of passion.

Adam pressed his hands against her back, down to the full curve of her hips, moving against her in a way that stirred her senses. His every touch was designed to entrance her, bring her deeper into his thrall with tempting promises of future delights. He kissed her face, her eyelids, and then her mouth a dozen times. Despite his ardor, there was an underlying gentleness in his embrace as he claimed her lips softly and with incredible sweetness.

The kiss, at first light and exploring, deepened to a sudden urgency, sending a rush of sensation cascading along her veins. She kissed him back with all the fervor she had repressed for those long, empty weeks. Waves of desire eddied through her, lapping insistently at her conscious mind until she gave herself up to the flood of joyous emotions. She was drowning in sensual pleasure, her body moving against his, begging to be swept away on the tide of their mutual need. He dragged his mouth from hers reluctantly, and his voice was shaky with longing for her as she untied the cape and let it fall around her feet.

"Ah, Cat Woman, you have me in your spell. Are you real, or will you disappear like the mist if I let go?" His hands roved over her breasts and down past her waist as if he sought to prove that she was indeed real.

Her hands were at his belt, loosening the catch. She wanted to feel him, all of him, every inch from head to toe, lying hard and warm against her. He flicked his belt open and pulled off his jeans, molding against her so that each curve and hollow of his body matched hers, as if they were made for each other in every meaning of the word. He caught her up in his arms, then knelt and lowered her to the ground, laying her on the satin lining of the cape.

"Oh, Cat! All the time we've lost because of foolish pride," he whispered hoarsely against the side of her throat.

"Adam, why didn't you answer my note?" She brushed her palms over his nipples, feeling them swelling and tightening with her insistent stroking. He didn't answer and Cat leaned forward, running the tip of her tongue along his chest, teasing and nibbling at his nipples until he arched his back and groaned. She nipped his earlobe next and softly repeated her question in his ear.

"Why do you always want to ask questions when we're making love?" he murmured, moving his leg between hers.

"Adam, I can't think when you do that," she began.

He cut off her words with the pressure of his mouth on hers as his hands explored the tender inside of her thighs with deliciously slow movements. Lightly his fingers brushed and circled, seeking even more intimate places. Once again Adam proved to Cat that he knew her body as well as she did, and soon the sensations she'd been trying to keep at bay grew stronger, more potent.

Every inch of her body had a heightened awareness of him, even the tickle of his warm breath on her soft skin. Cat felt as if she were floating away on a river of molten silver, her limbs all languorous and heavy. She wanted to carry Adam away with her on the surging tide of pleasure.

He brought her to the very crest of sensual ecstasy and she cried out, curving her hips up to meet his. She lost all awareness of what was Cat and what was Adam as their bodies joined, and then they were completely engulfed in the tidal wave of their surging emotions.

When the first rush of passion ebbed away, they were left on the shores of contentment in each other's arms.

They lay entwined, their bodies covered with a light sheen in the trellised shadows of the Eternity Tree, and they kissed and cuddled and whispered all the things that lovers do. Adam nibbled on her earlobe. "Where are your earrings? Don't you know it's illegal to lie around naked with nothing but a necklace unless you're wearing earrings, too?"

"I don't have any that go with this necklace. You'll have to make me some." She tickled the line of his jaw with the tip of her pink tongue.

"Well, I just happen to have the exact pair to match your eyes. They belong to you, you know."

For answer, Cat put her arms around his neck and drew him down again for a kiss that deepened quickly, as her tongue tangled sensuously with his. They kissed until they had to stop just to breathe.

Cat snuggled against his chest. "Now, as I was asking before, when I was so, eh, *marvelously* interrupted. Why didn't you answer my note? I waited and waited . . ." Her voice broke off in a gasp of pleasure as his hands teased one of her more vulnerable spots. She grabbed his wrist and laughed low in her throat. "No more of that until I get an answer from you."

"Because I *couldn't* write. I planned to send you a letter and tell you how I felt and ask you to come back. But I wanted to wait until after the surgery, and I just got the splint off my arm two days ago. And because I was stupid. I couldn't make head or tail of your note when it came. It seemed so . . . so cold and formal. I was too proud to ask someone else to write for me, in case you didn't answer . . . That's why I sent the necklace and belt you left behind. I thought you could read between the lines."

"Oh, Adam." Cat laughed. "And I thought you'd read between the lines of my note. Well, I'll never have to write you another letter."

"Why not?"

"Because I'm never going to leave you. 'Whither thou goest,' etcetera." She cradled his head against her breast while his hands resumed their assault on her defenses.

"Stop that," she said unconvincingly. "How can I talk to you while you're doing things that drive me crazy?"

"Don't talk," he suggested reasonably, continuing his raid on her citadel. He kissed her once, lingeringly. "You realize, of course, what this means? You'll have to marry me now."

"Of course," she teased back. "I'll do anything to get those earrings."

"You'll get those earrings. And a lot more." His

touch was more bold, and she moved against him with mounting eagerness.

"What will my name be when we're married?" Cat murmured against his skin.

"Oh, I'll still call you Heather Woman, and Cat Woman. Sometimes, Screeching Cat Woman. Ouch!" He rubbed his collarbone where she'd nipped him lightly. "And some people will call you Silversinger's Woman."

"I like the first and the last ones best."

"You know," Adam told her, resuming his previous actions, "we can't have you going back looking like this, with half your clothes missing. We'll have to stay here till it's good and dark." He kissed her breasts, then knelt, straddling her hips while his hands caressed and stroked and did delightful things to her body.

Cat stretched, smiling lazily up into his eyes. "What'll we do to pass the time?"

"We'll think of something, Tempting Cat Woman." Adam laughed back as she gave an involuntary gasp of pleasure. "We'll think of something. . . ."

GET SIX RAPTURE ROMANCES EVERY MONTH FOR THE PRICE OF FIVE.

Subscribe to Rapture Romance and every month you'll get six new books for the price of five. That's an $11.70 value for just $9.75. We're so sure you'll love them, we'll give you 10 days to look them over at home. Then you can keep all six and pay for only five, or return the books and owe nothing.

To start you off, we'll send you four books absolutely FREE. "Apache Tears," "Love's Gilded Mask," "O'Hara's Woman," and "Love So Fearful." The total value of all four books is $7.80, but they're yours *free* even if you never buy another book.

So order Rapture Romances today. And prepare to meet a different breed of man.

YOUR FIRST 4 BOOKS ARE FREE!
JUST PHONE 1-800-228-1888*

(Or mail the coupon below)
*In Nebraska call 1-800-642-8788

Rapture Romance, P.O. Box 996, Greens Farms, CT 06436

Please send me the 4 Rapture Romances described in this ad FREE and without obligation. Unless you hear from me after I receive them, send me 6 NEW Rapture Romances to preview each month. I understand that you will bill me for only 5 of them at $1.95 each (a total of $9.75) with no shipping, handling or other charges. I always get one book FREE every month. There is no minimum number of books I must buy, and I can cancel at any time. The first 4 FREE books are mine to keep even if I never buy another book.

Name _____ (please print) _____

Address _____ City _____

State _____ Zip _____ Signature (if under 18, parent or guardian must sign) _____

This offer, limited to one per household and not valid to present subscribers, expires June 30, 1984. Prices subject to change. Specific titles subject to availability. Allow a minimum of 4 weeks for delivery.

RAPTURE ROMANCE

Provocative and sensual, passionate and tender— the magic and mystery of love in all its many guises

Coming next month

A DISTANT LIGHT by Ellie Winslow. As suddenly as he'd once disappeared, Louis Dupierre reentered Tara's life. Was it the promise of ecstasy, or some unknown, darker reason that brought him back? Tara didn't know, nor was she sure whether she could risk loving—and trusting—Louis again . . .

PASSIONATE ENTERPRISE by Charlotte Wisely. Gwen Franklin's business sense surrendered to sensual pleasure in the arms of executive Kurt Jensen. But could Gwen keep working to prove she could rise as high as any man in the corporate world—when she was falling so deeply in love?

TORRENT OF LOVE by Marianna Essex. By day, architect Erin Kelly struggled against arrogant builder Alex Butler, but at night, their lovemaking was sheer ecstasy. Yet when their project ended, so did their affair, and Erin was struggling again—to make Alex see beyond business, into her heart . . .

LOVE'S JOURNEY HOME by Bree Thomas. Soap opera star Katherine Ransom was back home—and back in the arms of Joe Mercer, the man who'd once stolen her heart. But caught up in irresistible passion, Katherine soon found herself forced to choose between her glamorous career— and Joe . . .

AMBER DREAMS by Diana Morgan. Jenny Moffatt was determined to overcome Ryan Powers and his big money interests. But instead, his incredible attractiveness awed her, and she was swept away by desire . . .

WINTER FLAME by Deborah Benêt. Darcy had vowed never to see Chason again. But now her ex-husband was back, conquering her with loving caresses. If Chason wanted to reestablish their marriage, would his love be enough to help her overcome the past. . . ?

RAPTURE ROMANCE

*Provocative and sensual,
passionate and tender—
the magic and mystery of love
in all its many guises*

NEW Titles Available Now

(0451)

#33 ☐ **APACHE TEARS by Marianne Clark.** Navajo Adam Hawk willingly taught Catriona Frazer his secrets of silversmithing while together they learned the art of love. But was their passion enough to overcome the prejudices of their different cultures? (125525—$1.95)*

#34 ☐ **AGAINST ALL ODDS by Leslie Morgan.** Editorial cartoonist Jennifer Aldrich scorned all politicians—before she met Ben Trostel. But love and politics didn't mix, and Jennifer had to choose which she wanted more: her job or Ben .... (122533—$1.95)*

#35 ☐ **UNTAMED DESIRE by Kasey Adams.** Lacy Barnett vowed ruthless land tycoon Ward Blaine would never possess her. But he wore down her resistance with the same gentleness and strength he used to saddle-break the proudest steed ... until Lacy wasn't fighting his desire, but her own ... (125541—$1.95)*

#36 ☐ **LOVE'S GILDED MASK by Francine Shore.** A painful divorce made Merilyn swear never again to let any man break through her defenses. Then she met Morgan Drake.... (122568—$1.95)*

#37 ☐ **O'HARA'S WOMAN by Katherine Ransom.** Grady O'Hara had long ago abandoned the high-powered executive life that Jennie Winters seemed to thrive on. Could she sacrifice her career for his love—and would she be happy if she did? (122576—$1.95)*

#38 ☐ **HEART ON TRIAL by Tricia Graves.** Janelle Taylor wasn't going to let anyone come between her and her law career. But her rival, attorney Blair Wynter, was equally determined to get his way opposite her in the courtroom—and the bedroom ... (122584—$1.95)*

*Price is $2.25 in Canada

To order, use coupon on next page

RAPTURE ROMANCE

*Provocative and sensual,
passionate and tender—
the magic and mystery of love
in all its many guises*

 (0451)
- #19 ☐ CHANGE OF HEART by Joan Wolf. (124421—$1.95)*
- #20 ☐ EMERALD DREAMS by Diana Morgan. (124448—$1.95)*
- #21 ☐ MOONSLIDE by Estelle Edwards. (124456—$1.95)*
- #22 ☐ THE GOLDEN MAIDEN by Francine Shore. (124464—$1.95)*
- #23 ☐ MIDNIGHT EYES by Deborah Benét (124766—$1.95)*
- #24 ☐ DANCE OF DESIRE by Elizabeth Allison. (124774—$1.95)*
- #25 ☐ PAINTED SECRETS by Ellie Winslow. (124782—$1.95)*
- #26 ☐ STRANGERS WHO LOVE by Sharon Wagner. (124790—$1.95)*
- #27 ☐ FROSTFIRE by Jennifer Dale. (125061—$1.95)*
- #28 ☐ PRECIOUS POSSESSION by Kathryn Kent. (125088—$1.95)*
- #29 ☐ STARDUST AND DIAMONDS by JoAnn Robb. (125096—$1.95)*
- #30 ☐ HEART'S VICTORY by Laurel Chandler. (125118—$1.95)*
- #31 ☐ A SHARED LOVE by Elisa Stone. (125126—$1.95)*
- #32 ☐ FORBIDDEN JOY by Nina Coombs. (125134—$1.95)*

*Prices $2.25 in Canada

Buy them at your local

bookstore or use coupon

on next page for ordering.

RAPTURE ROMANCE

*Provocative and sensual,
passionate and tender—
the magic and mystery of love
in all its many guises*

(0451)
- #1 ☐ LOVE SO FEARFUL by Nina Coombs. (120035—$1.95)*
- #2 ☐ RIVER OF LOVE by Lisa McConnell. (120043—$1.95)*
- #3 ☐ LOVER'S LAIR by Jeanette Ernest. (120051—$1.95)*
- #4 ☐ WELCOME INTRUDER by Charlotte Wisely. (120078—$1.95)*
- #5 ☐ CHESAPEAKE AUTUMN by Stephanie Richards. (120647—$1.95)*
- #6 ☐ PASSION'S DOMAIN by Nina Coombs. (120655—$1.95)*
- #7 ☐ TENDER RHAPSODY by Jennifer Dale. (122321—$1.95)*
- #8 ☐ SUMMER STORM by Joan Wolf. (122348—$1.95)*
- #9 ☐ CRYSTAL DREAMS by Diana Morgan. (121287—$1.95)*
- #10 ☐ THE WINE-DARK SEA by Ellie Winslow. (121295—$1.95)*
- #11 ☐ FLOWER OF DESIRE by Francine Shore. (122658—$1.95)*
- #12 ☐ DEAR DOUBTER by Jeanette Ernest. (122666—$1.95)*
- #13 ☐ SWEET PASSION'S SONG by Deborah Benét. (122968—$1.95)*
- #14 ☐ LOVE HAS NO PRIDE by Charlotte Wisely. (122976—$1.95)*
- #15 ☐ TREASURE OF LOVE by Laurel Chandler. (123794—$1.95)*
- #16 ☐ GOSSAMER MAGIC by Lisa St. John. (123808—$1.95)*
- #17 ☐ REMEMBER MY LOVE by Jennifer Dale. (123816—$1.95)*
- #18 ☐ SILKEN WEBS by Leslie Morgan. (123824—$1.95)*

*Price $2.25 in Canada

Buy them at your local bookstore or use this convenient coupon for ordering.
THE NEW AMERICAN LIBRARY, INC.,
P.O. Box 999, Bergenfield, New Jersey 07621
Please send me the books I have checked above. I am enclosing $_____
(please add $1.00 to this order to cover postage and handling). Send check
or money order—no cash or C.O.D.'s. Prices and numbers are subject to change
without notice.

Name_____

Address_____

City _____ State _____ Zip Code _____

Allow 4-6 weeks for delivery.
This offer is subject to withdrawal without notice.

SPECIAL $1.00 REBATE OFFER WHEN YOU BUY FOUR RAPTURE ROMANCES

To receive your cash refund, send:

1. This coupon: To qualify for the $1.00 refund, this coupon, completed with your name and address, must be used. (Certificate may not be reproduced)

2. Proof of purchase: Print, on the reverse side of this coupon, the *title* of the books, the *numbers* of the books (on the upper right hand of the front cover preceding the price), and the U.P.C. numbers (on the back covers) on your next four purchases.

3. Cash register receipts, with prices circled to:
   Rapture Romance $1.00 Refund Offer
   P.O. Box NB037
   El Paso, Texas 79977

Offer good only in the U.S. and Canada. Limit one refund/response per household for any group of four Rapture Romance titles. Void where prohibited, taxed or restricted. Allow 6–8 weeks for delivery. Offer expires March 31, 1984.

NAME_____

ADDRESS_____

CITY_____STATE_____ZIP_____

SPECIAL $1.00 REBATE OFFER WHEN YOU BUY FOUR RAPTURE ROMANCES

See complete details on reverse

1. Book Title _____

   Book Number 451-_____

   U.P.C. Number 7116200195-_____

2. Book Title _____

   Book Number 451-_____

   U.P.C. Number 7116200195-_____

3. Book Title _____

   Book Number 451-_____

   U.P.C. Number 7116200195-_____

4. Book Title _____

   Book Number 451-_____

   U.P.C. Number 7116200195-_____